THE IMMORTAL EDGE

JON DEL ARROZ

1

No words could describe the beauty of the psychedelic blurs of light that made up hyperspace. Aristocrats paid handsomely for quarters with views of the unique sights of the physics-bending reality allowing travel between stars. Some even considered hyperspace to be a religious experience, a portal between God and man. There were no shortage of shamans, gurus, and fortune tellers who sold their insights to travelers along the stars of what they could divine from the radiant interstellar pools.

As a special agent of Terra Prime, Ayla Rin had her own hyperspace-capable ship. She didn't have to pay anything for the view from her cockpit. All she had to do was sit back and relax with her arms behind her head and enjoy the sights. Though, she did have to occasionally fight an artificial intelligence and his brainwashed armies culminating with a power-mad governor in mech armor. Details.

She'd just completed her mission on Laundar IV, saving the colonists from tyranny and restoring them to become loyal subjects of the Imperium. At least she had rid them of some of their problems. There would be an interim military governor installed from among the ranks of imperial generals to sort out the actual societal rebuilding of the world. Something beyond her pay grade.

Ayla rather enjoyed working with semi-autonomy, being able to fly on her own ship. She couldn't imagine a commission within the military system to play the game until one became a general to receive a political appointment. Some wanted power so much they'd devote decades to such careers. She'd also seen so many rise and fall due to scandals, or to having the wrong stance on an issue at the wrong time. Politics had to be a nightmare of a career.

Yet, her work involved politics in a way. Special agents like her kept the Imperium together without having to deal with the bloodiness of war—at least, most of the time. It wasn't to say she didn't have her fair share of fighting. She'd been genetically modified to increase her proficiencies in the hand-to-hand combat arena.

Jorus, her handler, had told her the reality when they'd first met.

"No one will suspect a buxom redhead would have the proportionate speed and strength of a professional gladiator. While they're distracted by your good looks, you can hit them with a one-two knockout." He'd laughed while saying it.

She supposed she should have been offended for having been chosen for the program due to her looks, but she wouldn't argue basic reality and human nature because she wanted to make some point on behalf of women. Men were visual creatures on average and, as a special agent, it was her duty to Emperor Grigor to use all of her assets to the Imperium's advantage.

She caught her reflection in the cockpit window, glimmering with the backdrop of a pool of light which exploded with reds and greens like a pebble had dropped into the pond of hyperspace reality. Her green eyes stared back at herself before the visual faded into brilliant light.

Bleep. Bleep. Bleep.

Her console alerted her to an incoming communique.

Ayla blinked a couple of times. She'd either fallen asleep or become hypnotized from the hyperspace light trails. How long had she been out?

"Mitis, who's calling?" Ayla asked to her AI assistant, named after the Greek mythological figure by Jorus, who thought 'giving her ship the Mitis touch' would be far cleverer than it was.

"Terra Prime Agency HQ," Mitis said in the AI's low, distinctly male voice, which sounded like an old-time audiowave announcer.

"Put it through."

"Ayla, I hope I wasn't interrupting your sleep cycle or anything," a voice said, one she recognized as Bethany Nava, Jorus's top aide. The girl had risen through the ranks of the organization fairly quickly, rumored to be "the next Ayla Rin" if the Imperium ever needed one.

It made Ayla grimace thinking of the contingencies her agency had in place in the event she suffered an untimely death. A harsh reality of her work.

"Bethany," Ayla replied in an all-too-sweet tone she'd trained herself to do when she didn't particularly want to talk but had to sound polite regardless. "Not at all. It's hard to sleep in hyperspace anyway."

"I feel you. I always have to take a sedative," Bethany said. "Jorus wanted me to call and check in on your progress toward Terra Prime."

Ayla glanced at her onboard star map to the upper-left of her cockpit console. "Looks like we're due to drop from hyperspace in another twelve hours."

"Right on time," Bethany said. "And your assets are secure?"

By assets, the woman meant Dr. Schantz, the artificial intelligence expert who had been integral in the development of OVERMIND. He'd given the AI supreme sentience, and it had almost succeeded in conquering Laundar IV. He was a brilliant scientist and, as such, needed strict oversight from the Imperium so nothing of the sort ever occurred again.

"He and his family are holed up in my quarters. They're safe and sound," Ayla said. If there were any danger of him being a flight risk or of someone kidnapping him again, the Imperium would have sent a fighter escort. Still, the Agency had to check on someone as important as Dr. Schantz as a courtesy. "Is there anything else?"

"One more thing. Jorus has a new mission brief to deliver to you, which he doesn't want to send over open comm lines. Apparently, there's more trouble brewing."

"There's always more trouble brewing." Ayla sighed. She was tired. This last mission took a lot out of her, both in the figurative sense because it was so physically taxing, and the literal sense because the techno-cultists who followed OVERMIND had drilled into her neck, extracted flesh, and inserted a virtual reality jack into her so she could plug into their ethernet. She needed to get it removed. Ayla wasn't tech-averse, but she didn't want to be part cyborg, either.

"Yes, but this is urgent."

"It's *always* urgent," Ayla said, unable to help but laugh under her breath. The Imperium was vast, composing of hundreds of planets. With trillions of humans spanned across them of all shapes, sizes, races, creeds, and genetic modifications. There was bound to be conflict and emergency happening full-time. It's why they had an intelligence agency on top of a robust space Marine corps.

"What I'm telling you is Jorus is requiring you to meet with him upon your arrival," Bethany said. Her voice became firmer. Maybe she was agent material after all. Not many people in the Agency stood up to Ayla. They feared her. As they should.

"I'm supposed to be due hazard leave," Ayla said. She was in no mood to meet, especially right after she touched down at Terra Prime. She wanted to go to her place, take a real shower, sleep, and spend a few days reading holo-novels in her garden to forget the Imperium's troubles. It's all she had.

With her life, she couldn't risk close friends or a family, or have any pets. It was solitary, with the reward being entirely within the work itself. Which meant she knew she would acquiesce and meet with Jorus, but she would still voice her bitterness for being called into duty so soon after such a difficult assignment.

"Accounting has authorized a credit payment of triple time for your last mission as compensation," Bethany said.

There, she had it. Always a carrot to follow the stick. One Ayla couldn't say no to. She could almost buy her own private luxury star yacht with all of the features of her agency-owned ship with that kind of money.

"All right, tell Jorus I'll meet him in the office."

"About that..."

Ayla crossed her arms over her chest. "Now what?"

"Jorus would like you to meet at the Rancher-Zeta Steakhouse in Mega-Austin."

"Mega-Austin is a long way from Agency HQ."

"He said it's the best steakhouse on Terra Prime."

Ayla shook her head. Jorus wanted to get her out to dinner. Typical. It also would be a good meal to expense to the agency, something he would take advantage of whenever he could. Always a schemer, which is how he came into a handler position to begin with. On the other hand, he had excellent taste in food. He knew how to dine, and how to bilk every last credit out of the agency on his expense account.

"Fine. Tell him I'll be there. I have to drop Dr. Schantz off in Imperiopolus first, though."

"I'll let him know you'll need a couple extra hours' travel time. Thank you."

"Ayla out."

She leaned her head back into her chair, less annoyed than she'd thought she'd be. She'd expected a new mission to come in upon her return, just not this quickly. The additional pay made it worth it, but she had to wonder what could get Jorus into such a flurry he couldn't wait to call her about it until she arrived.

Strange happenings occurred all over the Imperium. One couldn't say it was unexpected either, given there had been a thousand years of peaceful reign of a hegemony over the galactic region, with constant expansion. But there were too many planets under singular control now. They couldn't all be monitored all of the time. Too many colonies forged their own identities and cultures, which led to strange conflicts like the one she'd had on Laundar IV.

Ayla closed her eyes, despite the bright lights making it feel like her eyelids remained open. All she could do was hope there would be a simpler mission this time than the last.

2

DESPITE HER INSTRUCTIONS FROM BETHANY, AYLA WENT HOME TO HER apartment and showered. Jorus could wait. She came out in fresh clothes and took a flitter to New Austin Megacity, which added a couple of hours to her journey. Naturally, she'd had Mitis inform her office of the delay, which she cited as being unavoidable due to traffic. If Jorus wanted to meet her, she deserved a fresh change of clothes and a freshening up after a long flight.

She arrived at the steakhouse on top of a hundred story skyscraper, which was not even close to the tallest building along the megacity's skyline. Flitters, sky cars, and bikes zoomed past the windows in aerial traffic. Cross-traffic moved in a perpendicular direction a few levels below. Life was busy on Terra Prime, and Ayla didn't miss it.

She had to admit there was something charming about backwater worlds like Laundar IV. Sure, it had its metropolis, but it was far less busy than the seat of the Imperium. The galaxy revolved around this world, as it had for more than the thousand years since the Imperium was founded. The only place ever said to rival it was the original Earth, of which Terra Prime had been modeled and terraformed to be an exact replica of, after nuclear destruction had devastated humanity's original home beyond repair.

A blue-skinned maître d' stood at a podium at the front of the restaurant. He was bald, with an ocular implant on his right eye. He gave Ayla a once over.

She'd changed into a black dress, form-fitting, which was appropriate for a fancy restaurant and dining out. If Jorus wanted her in such a capacity, he'd have to deal with the whole place staring at her, as she knew they would. She let her crimson hair flow over her shoulders.

"Ayla Rin, here to see Jorus Stutengard," she said in her practiced sweet voice.

The man's eyes lingered on her for one more moment before he looked at the monitor embedded into his podium. He tapped on it. "Of course, here we are. This way, madame."

Ayla walked in high heels to follow the greeter to her table, hips swaying from the way her shoes forced her to move. Several men in the restaurant turned their attentions to her, which she noted but kept her eyes ahead to not encourage any potential suitors. She arrived in the best location along the window-line. Jorus didn't mess around when it came to quality leisure.

Jorus sat at the table, wearing a blue suit with a pointed lapel and a red tie. His attire came across as old-fashioned, but he liked to present himself as a part of the traditional Imperium, reminding others by his mere presence of the glory days of Terra Prime. If he had enough to drink, he could go on and on about it, which Ayla hoped to avoid this evening. She was tired enough after her long travels.

"You know, after the craziest mission you've ever sent me on, where some nut job governor had me surgically altered to be able to jack in to his ethernet virtual reality world, you have quite some gall to call me to some steakhouse for dinner," Ayla said, slipping into the seat across from him.

Jorus smiled back at her. "I like to think of it as my irresistible charm drew you to New Austin Megacity."

Ayla resisted rolling her eyes. "Hardly."

The waitress stopped by the table, Jorus ordering a bottle of wine that sounded expensive, though Ayla had no idea, before folding his hands on the table and turning his attention to her.

"Really, you will be delighted for this meal. It's the finest meat genetically replicated from authentic cows. Have you ever had real cow?"

"I try not to think about the animals I eat," Ayla said. He could be too enthusiastic about food. She enjoyed a fine meal well enough, but she would have preferred being back home. "Now, what is so important it couldn't wait?"

"All business and no fun with you." Jorus shook his head, making a *tsk* noise. He teased, and though he tried to make excuses to be in her company, he'd never been overly-aggressive or threatening to her. She wouldn't have put up with him had he been.

The waitress poured the wine and walked away, Jorus waited, looking after the woman through his glasses as she moved. He had an implant that would tell him when the waitress would be out of earshot, and it would be safe to speak. "Nanite filter," he said regardless, and a wall of soft light shimmered around them, dampening the sound from any possible listeners.

Ayla raised a brow at the precautions. "A public place and you're going to use anti-listening tech? Way to not draw attention."

"No one's watching us. I have camera drone monitors as well," Jorus said. He leaned back into his chair. "If you recall your last mission, it began with a lead that resulted in an entanglement with the Robeni pirates."

"How could I forget?" Ayla had almost been shot to death by pirates and had to escape by jumping through a window of a tall skyscraper. Fortunately, she'd had her jetpack or she might have never made it out alive.

"Turns out those pirates are back with a much bigger situation than before," Jorus said. He swirled his glass of wine then took a sip from it. "Still needs to open up a little."

Ayla swirled her glass similarly. "I still don't understand what the Nes Starliners had to do with the pirates and Laundar IV."

"This is why we send in a cleanup crew after you to retrieve more information," Jorus said, smiling. "As you know, we originally found comm logs tying Nes to Laundar IV and Project OVERMIND. We learned Nes wanted the OVERMIND AI tech for their starliner operation as a potential to replace pilots with an automated, interlinked network of a single intelligence. It would free up any potential traffic problems, plus it would be much less expensive to maintain than human pilots long-term.

"They funded much of the operation, as well as provided the intelligence of Dr. Schantz's location for the pirates for their kidnapping. Tidy, and we wouldn't have found all of the information to convict their board had you not blown the doors open on the Laundar IV insurrection."

Ayla sipped her wine. It tasted more like cherries than it did grapes, with a woody aftertaste to it. All in all, it didn't taste bad, but she didn't have nearly as much interest in the substance as Jorus did. She pushed the glass aside once it was on the table, not going to have more than a sip or two. Especially when they were talking missions.

"It all sounds tidily cleaned up," Ayla said. "What do you need me for now?"

Jorus took one more sip, and then the waitress returned. He paused the conversation, holding up a finger to tell both Ayla and the waitress to wait. "Do you mind if I order for us?" Jorus asked.

He was an old-fashioned sort and liked to pick the food when they went out. Ayla knew him well enough to trust his tastes. He enjoyed the finer flavors, especially when it was on the Imperium's credit account. "Sure."

"Two prime filets, then," Jorus said, offering over the digital menu to the waitress.

She collected them and left the table.

Jorus returned his attention to Ayla. "I need you to infiltrate the Robeni pirates."

Ayla laughed. "You have to be kidding me. They'll know I caught them on their last mission."

"Actually, all of the pirates were accounted for, blown up in the blast when you left the building," Jorus said. "No one is alive to know you were there."

It sounded far too dangerous for her to want to go on a mission like this. Pirates could be nasty sorts, and she didn't want to be caught out in the middle of nowhere in space with people who had no scruples. "I'm due for medical leave for this thing attached to my neck, and hazard vacation."

"You'll get it afterward. This is important," Jorus said.

"Why? Why can't it wait? Or can't you use another agent?"

Jorus shook his head. "You're the best we've got, plus Syrus is out on another assignment. It's more suited to a woman anyway. The pirates are, well..." He swiveled his glass again and looked at the wine, "thirsty."

"Gee, thanks," Ayla said, crossing her arms. She was being signed up to be ogled by the lowest of the low. How did she put up with this? "And what's so important that I'm needed to ship out to the pirates immediately?"

"There's rumors from the fringe worlds that there's a colony where they've found something that could destabilize the Imperium."

"Every mission you tell me the Imperium could be destabilized."

"This one's big, though," Jorus said. He paused and sipped his wine one more time. "The wine is opening nicely. You should try it again."

"I'm good. Spill the details."

Jorus played with the stem of his wine glass but looked at Ayla intently. "There are rumblings amongst the outer worlds of a new modified spore, which can bring about eternal life. Supposedly, it stops the cells from dying and deteriorating so one never ages."

"Sounds like something fanciful an old spacer might say about exploring uncharted worlds in the old days," Ayla said.

"It does, but there's enough rumblings where the Imperium has to take it seriously. As nice as eternal life sounds, there is a delicate balance to our society. If this works, and word of it spreads, the demand will be higher than production could possibly be from one planet. It would cause mass unrest, not to mention our theoretical sociological issues surrounding people not aging.

"Imagine if I never retired, and therefore never had need for a replacement. The young generation would grow up disgruntled, which would then lead to even more unrest. A fountain of youth sounds nice in theory but, in practice, it can devastate our way of life. That's before we even start thinking about the potential side-effects of such a spore in a human body."

Ayla narrowed her eyes, considering. She'd been genetically altered, and other such alterations existed to extend life already, but there were limits. People still couldn't help but taper off in their work once they hit eighty or ninety years old. Emperor Grigor was now in his thirties, and he would be able to serve for another fifty or sixty years before abdicating his throne to his eventual heir. The whole line of succession for all kinds of industries could be destroyed through a wonder drug causing people to never age.

She'd never thought of it. Being in her early twenties, Ayla had a long time before she would even consider the prospect of death. At least, by natural causes. People in her line of work didn't always have the lifespans others expected. The morose thoughts turned her to her wine, and she found herself taking a sip despite not wanting to drink much.

"If I'm following where you're going with this, the Robeni pirates must have some hold on this substance…a spore, you said?"

"Modified spore."

"And you want me to get in with them, find out where these spores come from, and I presume destroy all trace of it and ensure the pirates can't seize control of the production of this wonder cure for aging before they get a foothold and disrupt our society's way of life for their own profits."

Jorus smiled. "Got it in one. The agency has set you up to travel via starliner to the Ensabah Asteroid Field, an interesting social phenomenon where a planetoid that was not in orbit of a star was hit by a comet thousands of years ago, and they both broke up into small chunks of matter."

"Spare me the geo-spatial lesson." Ayla returned his smile with a sarcastic and fake one of her own.

"Apologies, of course. From there, you'll ingratiate yourself with the pirates and uncover their plans. Don't forget to check in along the way." He said those last words as if they were a warning.

"I couldn't report back from Laundar IV. The governor had communications jammed." Ayla crossed her arms over her chest.

"Well, you have your mission and know what to do." Jorus inclined his head toward a waitress who brought over their plates. The scent of grilled meat filled the air around them. "Now, let's enjoy our meal, shall we?"

Ayla picked up her fork with her left hand. Jorus raised his brow at her in response.

"What?" Ayla asked.

"You're left-handed?" He pointed to her fork with a knife in his right hand.

"Ambidextrous. Helpful on missions when I'm in tight spots." Ayla grinned.

"You're always full of surprises," Jorus said before cutting into his steak, the juices from the meat flowing out onto his plate.

3

THE LOEN 858 STARLINER ARRIVED AT THE ENSABAH ASTEROID FIELD after a three day journey which had forced Ayla to take a connecting flight at Trylar III. Even though the asteroid field was still technically Imperium-controlled space, as all mankind lived under the domain of the emperor, the perception of pirate ownership made it enough where Nes Starliners' corporate thought it would be politically advisable not to have a direct flight from Terra Prime.

Inconvenience aside, Ayla had a relaxing trip. The agency paid for a first class cabin, which gave her privacy along the journey, upgraded meals, and access to a virtual reality entertainment assortment—the last of which she didn't use. She'd had enough of virtual spaces to last her a lifetime. Even the thought of being jacked into OVERMIND's ethernet sent a chill up her spine.

The ship closed in upon one of the larger asteroids in the system, one with a sprawling structure protruding from it, which extended deep inside the asteroid. The structure had several prongs protruding from the asteroid, allowing for large vessels to dock without having to send landing shuttles into bays. Several such ships were already docked with the starbase while Ayla's transport slowly made its way in to connect.

This was as far as her agency would be of any help to her. As soon as she would set foot on the Ensabah Asteroid, she'd have no more backup, no more instructions. Ayla would be an independent contractor looking for work, trying to land a commission from the Robeni pirates.

She departed the ship with the other passengers, all in a line, scanning their idents into the base system as they passed through a small checkpoint. The Ensabah Asteroid was controlled by a loose corporate affiliation of several different companies, none of which wanted to take responsibility for safety. As such, the starbase and subsequent asteroid field around it had only minor security patrolling, enough to ensure no madman with a ray gun caused any problems among the local populace. Beyond obvious open criminality, anything went out here. A perfect safe haven for pirates.

With corporations being in charge, it also opened the local authorities to bribery. Ayla counted on being able to exploit some corruption, as she had done research on the way over, and identified the station director Marcus Olderman as a potential mark to get her acquainted with some of the pirates.

Her fake ident stated her to be a relative of the Kenak system's Duke, far from the line of succession. She determined she'd present herself as a bored aristocrat, looking for adventure, hoping to find some lucrative way to show up her family by making a living for herself outside their controls. It sounded like a plausible story.

Ayla managed to secure a meeting with Olderman, which she'd attend to after she found her way to guest quarters here. She pulled up a map on her visor glasses, which gave her directions down three levels and in the south wing of the station.

Ordinarily, she'd have attendants or bots help her, but she wanted to keep a low profile until she was ready to communicate with the pirates. She traveled the bowels of the starbase alone, keeping her eyes open in case anyone decided it would be a good idea to take advantage of a woman traveling without an escort.

No one bothered her along the way, and she arrived at a secure quarters, pressing her thumbprint to the scanner to open the door.

Station authorities had already keyed it to her identity, which gave her access to the space. Inside was a small bunk, a desk, a food processor, and a small refrigerator. Nothing fancy, but she didn't expect anything more from the pirates' stronghold. She set down her modest belongings and left once again to go meet with Director Olderman.

Ayla arrived at a level of corporate offices lining a hallway on a higher level of the asteroid, allowing a view out from the top into space. Lights shone from the rocks, illuminating the ships docked on the pylons as well as several other asteroids beyond the starbase floating in space. Some smaller rocks caught themselves in the base's shielding bouncing off an electrified grid, which sparked when they hit.

She entered a large waiting area with a circular reception desk. No one stood behind the counter, but a terminal display flashed to mark appointments. Ayla checked the meeting with Mr. Olderman, and it flashed green, instructing her to wait.

A humanoid-shaped bot on wheels arrived from a wall opening and stopped before her. "Mr. Olderman's office is this way."

It turned on its wheels, then zooming forward with the expectation of Ayla to follow. She walked down the corridor behind the bot until they arrived at a door, which automatically opened for the bot's presence, allowing Ayla entry.

Inside was a floor-to-ceiling window to space, allowing for one of the best views Ayla had seen since on the station. The office had a circular desk similar to the reception, but smaller, and a couple of modern art pieces of abstract shapes made out of metal. Olderman sat at his desk, his visor on, a holodisplay up where he moved figures across the air with a VR touchsense glove over his hand. He seemed distracted by his work at first, taking several long moments before he acknowledged Ayla.

"Ahh, Miss Rin, is it not? Or should I refer to you as Duchess Rin?" He lifted his visor and stood from behind his desk.

"Ayla is fine," Ayla said with a small smile. She'd put on the charm and, hopefully, he would be eating out of her hand. That's why Jorus hired her for the mission in the first place. Hopefully, he would be susceptible to such charms.

Olderman reached out his hand, and Ayla accepted with a semi-limp wrist to present herself as dainty to his much stronger shake. He slowly released her grip and returned to his seat, offering her a chair across from him.

"I understand you're looking for employment," he said, his eyes focused on her body as she took a seat, which had been her intention to accomplish, making sure to accentuate an arch in her back as she made her move before crossing her legs.

"I am," Ayla said. "Something adventurous. I don't mind taking a little risk and involving myself in some investment. I have capital."

Olderman narrowed his eyes at her. "Forgive me, but I don't get offers like this every day. The last time I had someone in here trying to get in on our operations, it turned out to be an Imperial agent trying to root out any potential illegalities here on the station."

Ayla maintained a smile. He'd have the same situation here, but she wouldn't give any indication of it being the case. It would be her job to convince him otherwise. "Well, my father on Kenak is an agent of the Imperium by his position, but that's exactly why I come here to try to divest myself from his tentacles—metaphorically speaking—wrapping around my body." She used the language intentionally to illicit the physical in Olderman's mind. It was all too easy to toy with these men sometimes.

"Well, we certainly wouldn't want that." Olderman rubbed his hands together. He shifted his eyes to the door as if to make sure they were in private. "I've had my people run your credentials before you arrived to confirm your identity, so we know you're the real deal. Can't fool imperial databanks."

Unless you *were* the Imperium. But Ayla didn't want to interrupt him. "Uh huh."

"My position as director here is granted to me because I'm a part of a larger consortium. You might have heard of us." He leaned in toward her and brandished a smug smile. "The Robeni pirates."

Ayla raised a brow at him. "I'd been expecting such. But I thought you might be on the outside with a contact, not part of them directly." He'd be sent to a detention cell as soon as she wrapped up this mission and made a report, but he didn't have to know that now.

"If people knew, it wouldn't be an effective cover. But I might be able to get you in on an operation if you don't mind leaving in a hurry. One of my trader ships is departing for a colony world that has all but been forgotten by the Imperium, Zenda. On Zenda, the people there have become insular over the centuries, but they also discovered a fungi which grows there that seemed to have extended their lives.

"Long story short, scientists have refined the property in this spore to be able to grant what we've always been looking for as humanity—a cure for death. I know it sounds far-fetched."

"I've heard of a lot of strange stories across the galaxy. I believe you. Wow. A cure for death. That could change everything." Ayla tried to look wide-eyed and impressed like she was some sheltered noble-woman making her way in a world far beyond her capabilities.

A smirk crossed Olderman's face. "I'm glad you think so. I do, too. I can certainly envision myself living forever. But we'll test it on a large enough sample size of the population to make sure it works before I do. Don't want to have any unforeseen complications. Science. It's a lovely thing."

"I'm sure," Ayla said dryly.

Olderman cocked his head at her. "Would you like a drink? I have a fine pinot from Aldebaran."

"I'm not well going to be able to drink and keep my wits about me enough to be able to work. Maybe when I get back from this mission?" Ayla fluttered her eyelashes just enough to look innocent.

Her display seemed to work well enough on Olderman, a man easily impressed by femininity.

"I suppose you're right. I'll hold you to that when you get back, though."

"Where will I be headed anyway?"

"Ah, yes. The details." He produced a datapad from his desk, tapping into it, and then offering it across the desk to Ayla. "Our ship, the *Peregrine* will be departing for Zenda, as I said. She'll be under the command of Captain Mihael, one of our finest in the fleet. He'll be heading to the planet to verify the authenticity of this wonder drug as well as to procure samples if it proves to work. We don't know much about this planet because it has been so off the radar for so many years, but based on our preliminary observations, they are friendly to our business enterprises."

Ayla took the datapad, looking at the ship information as well as her credentials as a member of the crew. This all went easily. She'd had her assignment and identity, and everything had gone forward without a hitch. She knew better than to expect such luck to hold for much longer on one of these missions, but it could be a simple open and shut case. She had data on the pirates, confirmation of Olderman running these operations, but if these facilities with this anti-death drug were real, she would need to destroy them. She took a deep breath.

"Something wrong, my dear?" Olderman asked.

"Just nerves," Ayla said. "Nothing I can't handle."

"Good. I'll look forward to your return. As you'll find on the datapad, this will lead to handsome compensation if you are successful. Welcome to the Robeni pirates."

4

AYLA TRACKED CAPTAIN MIHAEL TO A LOCAL BAR ON THE FOURTH LEVEL known as The Outpost. It looked dirty and dingy like any number of spaceport dive bars she'd been to over the course of her career. The Outpost had metal plated floors and tables made of much the same material without much thought put into the design. People had scratched their names into the walls and tables with sharp objects, and it had the distinct air of a place that hadn't seen a deep cleaning.

Regardless of how sanitary The Outpost was, more than enough people gathered there. If a bar offered libations and at good enough of a price, people tended to ignore how nice an establishment could be.

Ayla hadn't had time to go through any databanks. She didn't know what the pirate captain looked like. In her imagination, Mihael would have a scruffy beard, unkempt, oily face, and scraggly hair. Though he didn't have to be a picture of a fantasy pirate, he could be anyone.

Several men gathered at the bar, laughing, clanking their beer steins together. It seemed a good a place to start as any. Ayla walked up to the bar, leaning against it, slipping between a couple of the men, and facing one of them. It was an aggressive move, but sure enough to get attention.

The man facing her gave her a quick once over, trying to be subtle but, under the influence of alcohol, he couldn't hide his gaze. "New 'round these parts?"

Ayla smiled weakly. "How could you tell?"

"Something about you. Your clothes, maybe. White isn't a popular color 'round here," the man said.

"Why not?"

"Tends to get stained."

"By work in the asteroids? From the dirt?"

"From blood."

She'd entered into a dangerous place. Ayla was aware of the proclivities of pirates, but it didn't faze her. She motioned to the bartender and ordered herself a beer, not that she particularly wanted to drink one, but she wanted to fit in and be one of the proverbial boys.

"What's your name?" the man asked, turning back toward the bar and taking a sip of his beer. He tried to act casual, but Ayla was trained well enough to notice a man's interest in her.

"Ayla. You?"

The bartender slid a stein across the table to her.

"Zahn," the man said.

"Nice to meet you, Zahn. I could use a few friends out in the fringes," Ayla said.

"Where you from?"

"The Kenak system," Ayla said, executing her cover identity without hesitation.

"That's a long way off." Zahn huffed. "And a really nice place." He turned back toward her, scrutinizing her more closely. "Don't see a lot of your types out here."

Ayla tried to laugh it off. "What do you mean by *your types*?"

"Rich people. I've been to Kenak. It's a nice planet, and nice ladies don't just make their way to Ensabah. Something must have happened."

She tried to maintain a cheerful twinkle in her eye. "I've got a history. I'm sure we all do here. Maybe a story for another time."

"Hmph," Zahn grunted, burying his face in his stein once more. He came up for a burp.

The conversation died pretty quickly, with no real opening for Ayla to say much else. It wouldn't matter. If she tried to talk to him, he'd pay her attention. Zahn couldn't stop shifting his eyes toward her to catch more glances. He lacked the confidence to try to keep the conversation going.

Before she could find another topic, the sound of two men arguing distracted her. They shouted curse words at each other, and it looked to be escalating. The bartender waved to try to distract them from each other and separate them. It appeared to be working.

"I never understood why people would go into a bar, a place where you can get drinks to take the edge off and feel good, and then get aggressive," Ayla said.

Zahn shrugged. "Some people get angry when they're drunk. The captain gets this bug in him tellin' him everyone is out to get him or slight him. Only when he's had a few too many, though."

"Captain…" Ayla repeated. Her ears perked at the word. It was a slim chance, because there had to be a large number of freighter captains aboard the station, but she'd been lucky so far. "Wouldn't happen to be Mihael by chance?"

Zahn furrowed his brow. "How'd you know?"

"Lucky guess." Ayla's smile grew. "I've been assigned to his ship. Some of the hired muscle, I think."

"You don't look like much muscle," Zahn said, which gave him an excuse to look her over again.

"Looks can be deceiving. I've had genetic mods." She looked up over him to the other two men who still seemed to be bickering. One of them had a beard, not the scraggly kind she envisioned in a pirate, but a tight one covering his chin with a thin line connecting to his brown hair. Of the two, he was the one who looked the most like a captain. His jawline was rigid, a defined bone structure to his cheeks. She could consider him a leader. The other man had a rounder face, while not obese, he had a few more pounds than he probably should have if he were in good shape. "Captain got a beard?"

"Nope," Zahn said.

Surprising. But then, Ayla had just said looks can be deceiving. She focused on the man with the rounder face. He had green eyes, light brown hair, and he seemed to wobble like he was barely able to keep himself up.

"You don't talk that way about my mother!" Mihael shouted, and that was the last of words defining the exchange. He balled a fist, drew it back, and popped the bearded man right in the mouth.

The action only caused another table of ruffians to get up, heading over to defend their friend. Zahn slid back from his stool as well.

"Love to chat more, but looks like the cap's in trouble," he said. The pilot moved with incredible speed to intercept the ruffians from the other table, taking his barstool with him, pulling it up, and smacking one of them upside the head with it. The stool resounded with a *crack*, and the man fell limp to the ground. His other two friends backed away.

It left the captain in a fistfight with the bearded man. Both of them had their dukes up, circling each other around the bar and looking for an opening. They seemed to have at least a basic understanding of boxing, keeping a guard, jabbing lightly when they could without opening themselves up to too much damage. Both, however, had drank too much and stumbled more than they could maintain their footing.

This was ridiculous, but Ayla didn't want to draw attention to herself. She slinked away from the bar and closer to the exit, keeping an eye on the events transpiring.

Zahn swung his chair around as a deterring weapon, keeping the other two ruffians at bay while the boxing match transpired.

"Security!" the bartender shouted. But no one was around to come to the call, at least for the time being.

Mihael gave up any pretense of a boxing match, driving the full weight of his body into the bearded man and slamming him into the bar. It knocked the wind out of his opponent. Mihael then threw one more punch to the man's face, connecting hard to his nose. With the alcohol already dulling senses, it was enough to cause the man to fall over.

It hadn't been an elegant fight, but at least he'd won cleanly. A wide grin across his face told how proud he was of the exercise.

"We should get out of here before we have to deal with security," Zahn said.

"I was just closin' out my tab anyway," Mihael said. He dropped a couple of credit chits on the bar and swaggered toward the door. Zahn kept pointing his stool at the other ruffians, making sure his captain was covered.

Ayla watched with amusement, crossing her arms over her chest. Whatever this insult the bearded man had delivered had better have been worth it. Though, she supposed it was none of her business, as long as they departed the station as they were supposed to tomorrow.

Zahn backed toward the door, but the men didn't seem like they were pursuing. Mihael stumbled over and Ayla pushed herself off the wall, taking Mihael by an arm.

"Oh, ho. Impressed with my fighting?" Mihael asked, all too happy to see her.

"Hardly. I'm just assisting my future captain so he doesn't screw up the mission before it starts," Ayla said.

They walked together, or at least she walked, and he stumbled, and made their way out of the bar into the corridor. Despite it being the same recycled air from the starbase's environmental systems, it seemed fresher. There was less of a stench of drunk men out here, even with one so close to her that Ayla felt him breathing on her neck.

Zahn stepped up along the other side. "Thank you for helping," he said.

"No problem," Ayla said.

Zahn was cogent enough to lead them back around to the docking pylon where their ship had been secured. Several other of the crew lounged about the recreational areas of the vessel. They ended up in a lounge with a few comfortable chairs where Ayla let go of Mihael and allowed him to flop onto one of the cushions.

"Ah," Mihael exhaled.

"I'm surprised you made it back in one piece," one of the pirates across the room said—a man with darker skin and a suit, which looked like a gray suede material. He had a sense of style, or at least liked to appear like he did.

"Nonsense, Rams, I'm fine," Mihael said.

"Regardless, we made it back. The crew of the *Hydra* were starting their nonsense again," Zahn said, taking a seat near to Mihael.

"I hope you whooped them good," Rams said, taking out what appeared to be a stick of chewing gum from one of his pockets and popping it into his mouth. "Who's the broad?"

"New crew," Zahn said. "She says she's muscle?"

Rams laughed at Zahn's words.

Ayla didn't care. She didn't need to posture or prove herself. She knew her capabilities and would demonstrate them in due time.

"The dear woman helped me here." Mihael smiled up at her. "I owe you a debt."

Ayla had an amused expression on her face. "Nonsense. Let's make some money from this mission, and we'll never have debts again, hmm?"

"What do you know about it?" Mihael asked.

"Olderman told me everything," Ayla said. At least, she thought he had. She liked to use nonspecific language in situations like this because it encouraged the others to open up about details she might have missed.

"I'm sure he left out the part about the fringe regions of space being dangerous," Zahn said.

"Won't be too dangerous for this ship," Mihael mumbled in a drunken stupor. His eyes opened and closed slowly a couple of times. It appeared he wasn't long for the world of the conscious.

"What do you mean?" Ayla asked, trying to sound innocent enough.

"Ships have been disappearing out along the fringe," Rams answered. He chewed a few times. "There's rumors of aliens."

Zahn shook his head. "I'm not sure I believe that. The Imperium's lasted for more than a thousand years in space. If aliens were out there, we'd have seen them by now."

"Or they're waiting for the right moment, analyzing us, making sure they can destroy us before they make their move," Rams said.

The seriousness of his words sent a shiver up Ayla's spine. She'd heard about the possibility of aliens before. Intelligence had enough unexplained phenomena to where anything could be out in the black. But she didn't want to be the one to have to discover them and run into strange monsters. "Well, we know our destination. It should be a simple trip. Maybe we should hold off on the aliens talk until we're sobered up. How about one of you gentlemen show me to my quarters so I can get settled and freshened up?"

Both Zahn and Rams moved, stared at each other, but then Rams went back to leaning against the wall, deferring to the pilot.

"This way, m'lady." Zahn motioned toward the door.

5

Ayla settled into her bunk. The pirates seemed like nice enough people, as far as criminals went. As a reasonably attractive woman, it made it easier to settle into any group, except among other women. The petty bickering and jealousy got to her some of the time, which left her with few friends over the years, though her career choice often left her with fewer.

Sometimes, she wondered if she made the wrong decision, if she'd be happier with a normal life, which left her close to home, but when she had been given the opportunity at the time to become genetically modified and enter the program, she became indebted to the agency.

It was too late to regret her life while she laid on a bunk in a cabin of the Robeni pirate ship, *Peregrine*. The quarters had no view into space, situated in the center of the vessel in case of any problems with decompression. Ship designers figured those with cheap vessels didn't want to risk losing crew in their sleep. Ayla understood why, but also knowing how little was spent on the construction of trader ships like the *Peregrine*, she could hardly rest easy while on the move.

It left her awake with her thoughts. She decided to pick up her datapad to read, learn a little more about the planet Zenda before they arrived. It never hurt to be more prepared and to have a better understanding of one's environment.

The planet was approximately one third of the size of earth, with point nine five gravity, which would give the sensation of feeling a little lighter, but not too noticeable of a difference. It had natural water formations, which is why it had been researched by the Imperium more than fifteen hundred years ago for potential settlement.

Zenda had more than four thousand species of identifiable plant life, though the last registered team looking into the site was from more than a millennium ago. It had several identifiable insects, but no mammalian life forms. The oddest thing Ayla found, was the planet had a human population listed as zero.

It had to be a mistake. She tried to cross reference Zendans or Zenda Colony but found nothing. This was the only entry. Olderman had been right about this being lost to the Imperium. How could a whole society exist without the bureaucracy knowing about it? There were too many planets, too many colonies to keep track of. It was almost too much for one government to bear.

She'd heard the argument before about how the Imperium should split into two and not be controlled by a single emperor, but those arguments sounded treasonous to her. It just meant they had to have better data and get these fringe colony worlds under control.

The fringes always caused the problems. It was hard to have too much crime or rebellion if the world was one within the core center of the Imperium. The closer a world was to Terra Prime, the easier it would be dispatch some of the fleet to quell grumbling populaces. The Imperium had a robust military, but it was rarely deployed because there were no enemies capable of fighting against it.

There had been civil wars in the past, but the last one was over five hundred years prior. The Imperium has had a long time of peace, which had led to too many people getting lazy and put the whole of the Imperium in decline.

It wasn't a positive thought, but it was also why Ayla had a job. She would take care of the problems others couldn't. They'd given her the power and the authority to do so.

But, for some reason, she dreaded her assignment here more than several of her past ones. Usually, she'd had her AI with her, her ship, a whole host of gadgets. Here, she had only a bag she could carry, and she was trapped in a tin can with pirates who she couldn't trust when push came to shove. Would they even care about being loyal subjects? They didn't seem hostile to the emperor, but their entire existence flew in the face of law and order.

Ayla sat up, careful not to hit her head on the top of the railing of the cabin. The ceiling was low in here, to conserve cargo space for the rest of the ship. The quarters were meant for sleeping only, no other functional use.

She decided to head back out into the corridor. Even though it was a late hour by station local time, someone had to be up or on shift around the pirate vessel. Perhaps even Captain Mihael had recovered from his alcoholic bender. He would have had to have had a mad hangover, or at least taken some hypo in order to mitigate it. She couldn't say she felt particularly bad for him with how much he had drunk.

The corridors were thin, again only for a functional movement between places rather than meant for any comfort. Several of the lights were out along the corridor, which only added to Ayla's fears about maintenance and general repair of the pirate vessel. Didn't these people take any care for the hunk of metal keeping them alive and safe from the vacuum of space?

It could have used a woman's touch, as much as she hated the cliché.

She found her way to the galley, which opened into the lounge where she'd spent time with the others earlier in the evening. A few pirates gathered around a long bench-shaped table, ones she hadn't recognized. They paused their conversation to stare up at her, and they didn't look too friendly.

Ayla greeted the suspicious stares with a smile. "Hello, I'm Ayla. New to the ship. I suppose I will have to prove my worth to the crew?"

A woman laughed, the only other female Ayla had seen among the crew so far. "With a figure like yours, I doubt there will be much complaining about you." This woman had a thin frame to her, with long, brown hair and pronounced red lips. She could have easily been competition for men's attention over Ayla.

"I appreciate the compliment, though I hope to add more value to the crew than being a pretty face." She stepped over and offered her hand to the woman, ignoring the men with her for the moment. "My name's Ayla."

"Tanya," the other woman said. She eyed Ayla's hand with skepticism but finally took it. "Welcome to the *Peregrine*."

"And your friends?" Ayla motioned her head toward the men with her.

Rams, the ruffian she had met before was there with them. "I don't know that I'd call her a friend."

Tanya punched the haggard man in the side. "Shut up, Rams."

Another man, who appeared to be in his late teens, lanky like a string bean with blond hair smiled at Ayla. "Jannik."

At least one of them was friendly. The others, well, she could work on them. Some people took time. A pirate's life had to have been one of betrayal and treachery.

"Zahn seems to like you, but I don't trust you," Rams said, as if ready to personify doubt in her. "I heard you were a princess."

"Duchess," Ayla corrected.

"What's that?" Jannik asked.

"It's not quite royalty. I don't think the emperor would take too kindly to people calling themselves a royal family on planets," Ayla said diplomatically. It was an understatement. If the emperor found a king or queen out there, they'd be executed.

Tanya chuckled. "Either way, what are you doing with a group of pirates? Shouldn't you be out sipping tea and sampling your personal chef's pastries?" She had a tinge of jealousy to her voice despite her laughter.

"I found the cushy life isn't for me," Ayla said, helping herself to a seat at the rally bench. Even though she hadn't been invited, she was firmly within conversation now and wanted to be among them. "Besides, I want to prove myself and make my own money. My father can't control me if I'm self-made."

"Well, you're an idiot to come to the pirates. Only the captains get rich, if then. Mihael drowns himself in liquor too much to be much of a use in getting us anywhere," Rams grumbled.

Dissent among the ranks? Ayla took note, careful not to make her own judgments and alienate them. The social situation was already tepid with all eyes on her. It felt as if they were waiting for her to give a signal where she could be identified as a traitor. Not a great position for someone who was here as an undercover spy. She had to do all she could to try to diffuse their suspicions.

"He's not so bad," Jannik said. "He's paid me on time, at least."

Tanya shrugged. "You're not getting rich on your deckhand pay. You don't even have a proper share yet."

"Neither do you," Jannik said.

Ayla had been offered an eighth share straight away. In fact, she had no stipend but would be participating in all of the profits from the venture. It was a gamble, one worthy of a duchess—if it were truly her identity. She could only imagine relying on meager pay from a pirate operation to try to scrape by. It made her chest ache for these people, but she wouldn't let herself get attached and spoil the mission.

"I find it odd a duchess would lower herself to this, even if it is what you say. Doesn't feel right," Tanya said.

"Why would she lie?" Jannik said. "She looks pretty enough to be a princess, anyway. At least not one of us. Look at her fingers. They're smooth not calloused."

Ayla tried her to not scoff at them analyzing her appearance, but she had to play nice. "I assure you, I'm not proud of my situation."

"And if you fail, you can always run home to daddy and beg forgiveness. You don't know what this life is like." Tanya looked away, becoming distant all of a sudden.

If they had been alone, Ayla would have been able to console her, but with the other two men here, she doubted she'd be able to make a real personal connection. "I won't lie, I have a safety net. But I want to make it on my own and prove myself. I'll work hard. You won't be carrying any dead weight with me."

Jannik smiled. "Seems all right to me."

"You just think she's pretty," Rams said.

"Prettier than your mug for certain," Tanya said.

Friendly ribbing seemed to dial down the tensions to some degree.

"Hey, I was looking into this planet we're supposed to go to, Zenda. Did you know the imperial databanks have it listed as uninhabited? Why do you think it's off the records?"

"Lots of planets like that out on the fringes. Imperial agents can't be everywhere to take a census," Rams said. "Stranger still is the Floating City. It's made up of several abandoned freighters who flew out too far over the last thousand years. It's where I'm from. It looks like an abomination—"

"Much like you," Tanya said.

Rams snorted. "Quiet. But it's my home. It's not on the star charts either."

Red lights flashed in the galley. Ayla perked, looking up. "What's that mean?"

"We're about to drop from hyperspace," Jannik said, sliding out from his spot on the bench to stand. "I'd better man my post at the rear cargo ramp."

"And I'd best check on the engine room," Rams said. "Not that there'll be any need for engines now. Mihael likes to have his tech on standby anyway." He followed Jannik in standing and both of them made their way out of the room without further goodbyes.

"What about you?" Ayla asked.

Tanya picked up her glass off the table and raised it toward Ayla. "I'm the ship's cook. I'm right where I'm supposed to be."

6

Ayla hadn't been given an official duty position on the ship as of yet. She kept saying she would act as hired muscle, but Olderman had only assigned her to a berth aboard the *Peregrine*, no official duties. Captain Mihael hadn't been helpful in being able to discuss ship's duties or to have any cogent conversation at all.

Jannik had said he'd be heading to the rear cargo bay to operate the ramp. Upon landing, the other pirates would have to exit the ship somehow, and it seemed like it would be easiest from there. It seemed a good a place as any to stand around and wait for an opportunity to join the crew in an official capacity.

The ship landed, the walls rattling when it touched down. From her position in the galley, Ayla couldn't see the landscape outside.

She left the galley, weaving through the small corridors and making her way back to the cargo bay. Sure enough, Jannik stood at the controls. Rams leaned over his console, engaged in conversation with the younger pirate. They stopped their conversation to look up at her.

"You'll be going to the meeting then?" Rams asked.

"Hello to you, too," Ayla said. She hadn't been made aware of any meeting, but it always paid to take initiative. "And yes. Hired muscle. In case something goes wrong."

Rams stood up straight, nearly a head taller than her and much sturdier. If Ayla hadn't had genetic enhancements, he would have been able to snap her in half without breaking a sweat. "Muscle, hmm? Always been my job before."

"Leave her alone, Rams," Captain Mihael said, stepping through the doorway into the cargo bay.

Rams grunted but took a couple of steps away from her.

Mihael sized her up. "You sure someone of your pedigree can handle a strange world? We don't know whether these people will be hostile."

"I know my way around a laser blaster," Ayla said. She didn't need to sound confident. She'd probably had more experience in combat than this entire crew combined.

It seemed to be enough for the captain, who nodded to her words. "Good. We'll be heading to a local watering hole called the Shamrock Pub. Something from original Terra culture, I don't know. It's supposed to be a brief walk from the spaceport, so we shouldn't run into too many problems."

"I can try to learn about local customs along the way," Ayla said. Keeping a low profile had to be one priority, but she also had to make herself valuable to these pirates if she wanted to get herself into a position where she could take control for her real operation.

Rams sneered. "Just keep quiet and do what you're told, princess."

It seemed people calling her "princess" would be making the rounds. "Duchess," Ayla corrected.

"We don't need fighting between us," Mihael said, much more cogent when he was sober. "We'll have to keep our eyes peeled and make sure we stay safe. I'll handle our contact with the Zendans. Jannik, lower the ramp, and let's get out of here."

Jannik took the captain's words as an order to lower the ramp, and he tapped the controls. The back wall of the cargo bay descended, clicking along the way as it moved in steps. It revealed an outside world with a pink sky, and a nearly empty spaceport. Zenda didn't appear to have many offworld travelers, which made sense, as the place was listed as uninhabited in the imperial databanks. Still, a few other ships lined the tarmac, some connecting to portals around in buildings that were shapped like bubbles.

The skyline beyond had more buildings, almost circular in their geometries but with flat surfaces around it forming different angles. The buildings had solar panels, woefully out of date for their power sources, but then this colony hadn't been visited for hundreds of years. It would be a backward place.

Several flitters flew through the sky, but no traffic like Terra Prime. This was a smaller city compared to any of the metropolises Ayla had visited back home.

A ground car arrived at the back ramp. It had a windshield with no top with room for three or four to sit and had a man sitting at a control panel. He looked up. "Taxi service. Take you where you need to go."

Mihael stepped forward. "Just what we needed. I'm looking to go to the Shamrock Pub. Can you take us there?"

The man tapped in the title into his system, which pulled up a map on his display. He confirmed the coordinates and looked back up. "Simple enough. What kind of payment you got?"

"Imperial Grigorums?" Mihael asked.

The man didn't look super pleased by it, but he seemed to accept it anyway. He motioned to the car. "Get in."

Mihael slid into the back first, followed by Rams, and Ayla took the right-hand side. Jannik stayed at his control console, shutting the ramp after they'd exited. Once they were in the car and seated, the automatic driving function took off.

"They have a pilot to input where to go and that's it?" Ayla asked.

"Driver not pilot. And yes. I wouldn't know how to move this thing myself. I'm also here in case we need to stop in case of emergency." He motioned to a lever by his right hand, which was bright red and had lettering on it saying, "Pull to Stop." It seemed simple enough.

Ayla wondered why it wasn't automated. She knew some piloting required human hands because of too many decisions to be made, but this ground car seemed to follow a simple route.

It sped along the tarmac and out to a narrower speedway beyond. It had rails on either side, which zoomed by in a blur as they moved at quick speeds. They took an exit ramp down into an area dense with those bubbled buildings, onto busy streets where the inhabitants seemed to be.

The car slowed, allowing Ayla a view of the streets. Dozens of people were in similar ground cars or walked along sidewalks, some having display glasses like Ayla's, seeming to be activated, and others looking at handheld electronics. No one seemed to be without them, a stark contrast from Terra Prime where not everyone seemed to be so plugged in all of the time.

It reminded Ayla of Laundar IV and the ethernet where the colonists had all jacked into the OVERMIND's virtual reality. Hopefully, she wouldn't have to deal with a rogue artificial intelligence here.

They arrived at a brown, bubble-shaped building with a sign hanging from it which said, 'Shamrock Pub.' The sign was in green and had the shape of a clover around the lettering.

Mihael thanked the man, debited his Grigorums, and the three of them stepped out onto the sidewalk in front of the pub. Mihael looked back at Ayla and Rams. "Remember, I do the talking."

The group walked inside, noting people sitting at sparse tables and an empty bar. It was a stark contrast from the pirate base that had buzzed with travelers. Zenda, being off any official documents, wouldn't get too many tourists. Many probably didn't even know anyone lived here.

Ayla paced lackadaisically, trying to seem like any natural traveler. She moved to the bar with Rams beside her. Mihael intercepted a server.

"What's your best drink?" Mihael asked.

The server, a blonde woman with long hair, stopped to tilt her head curiously at Mihael. She had a chip protruding from her skull by her left eye. She paused, canting her head as if processing something. "Retrieving most popular items," she said.

"You don't have a recommendation?" Mihael asked.

"Processing."

A few moments passed, and the blonde woman's eyes lit up. "Our Julep Kick is very popular."

Mihael raised a brow.

"It's a mint-flavored drink," Rams said.

Mihael made a disgusted face, scrunching his nose. "Get me an ale."

"Very well, sir," the woman said, turning to fill a stein from a tap.

One of the locals seemed to take note of Ayla from a table of men. He gave her a small smile. Ayla inclined her head toward him. Might as well use her looks to be able to get some information from the people here.

The man took her eye contact as an invitation, and he stood from his seat, sauntering over to her. Mihael received his drink about that time, and Rams rattled off an order to the waitress, but Ayla was too distracted by the incoming local to hear what he'd gotten. The man had brown hair, dark skin, and dark eyes. He stood a little shorter than her.

"You're an offworlder?" the man asked.

Ayla batted her eyelashes. "What makes you think that?"

He motioned to her clothes. "No one wears white around these parts."

"Why not?"

He paused, and Ayla noted he had the same chip on the left side of his skull as the waitress had. "It's the color of the dead."

"Old tradition?" Ayla asked. "I hope I'm not offensive."

"Not offensive, just unusual. I had to ask my processor unit what it meant. I just hadn't seen it in recent memory."

These processor units weren't completely uncommon. Ayla had seen them before. She preferred to have her retinal scan tech through her visor, which she wore over her eyes. That way she could take it off.

Even though the technology was said to be safe, she appreciated the ability to disconnect—now more than ever, since she'd seen the dangers of being fully connected to an artificial intelligence. A brainwashed population on Laundar IV gave her pause from using any ethernet connection.

But these people were also looking up mundane items they should have known. A waitress should have recommendations for a popular drink. This man should know why a color was a social faux pas to wear. Why did they have to pause to find such obvious information?

"What's your name?" the man asked.

"Ayla."

"That's a pretty name." He twitched as if storing something in his mind. Something was off about him, that was for certain. "I'm called Dorrinal."

The bar doors opened, and a bald man in a gray suit entered, followed by a couple of strongmen. All three of them had the chips on the sides of their face much like the patrons Ayla had noted. Did everyone on this planet share the implant? It seemed suspicious. She found herself unconsciously touching the jack port on her neck, the place where OVERMIND had forced her to enter his ethernet matrix.

The AI had done everything in its power to brainwash her. Fortunately, she had undergone the psych training from the agency to be able to resist it. But what if something stripped away her memories? How would she be able to function? It unnerved her to think about.

The bald man took note of Mihael, and the two men spoke to each other. Ayla turned toward her other companions, distracted from the conversation, missing what the man with her said.

Rams inclined his head toward her. "Hey, princess. Our meeting's here. Stop your flirting and let's get to business." He stood with Mihael and the three men who just entered, making his way over to a booth in the corner of the restaurant.

Ayla slid off her stool, standing poised as she could. She gave the man beside her a warm smile. "Duty calls. Nice to meet you."

"Will I see you again?" Dorrinal asked. He had clearly become more enamored with her in that moment than she had realized, his eyes hopeful.

"Who knows? It's a big galaxy." She sauntered over to the rest of her group. This mission might be over quickly if she'd be getting information about this strange chemical. One could only hope. She could use a peaceful rest back on Terra Prime, volunteering to help tend the Imperial Gardens. It sounded much nicer than this strange planet.

7

The bald man took a seat, looking rather comfortable despite having two tough thugs on either side of him. Opposite them, Rams sat on one side of Mihael with Ayla on the other. She observed the locals closely, perfectly content with the captain's orders to let him do the talking. It let her do her job for the Imperium without interruption.

"My name is Zarmol," the bald man said, extending his hand across the table. "I presume you are of the Robeni?"

Mihael nodded and took the man's hand and shook is. "Captain Mihael. It's good to meet you in person. We've exchanged several text-based communiques. I was surprised we'd been unable to have any onscreen conversations."

"Something in our atmosphere makes connectivity for video transmissions to become unstable. I apologize," Zarmol said.

"Mm," Mihael said. It sounded like he didn't buy it.

Ayla didn't much believe the man either. He seemed a little too slick and polished with his answers. As if he'd been pre-programmed. She'd dealt with similar on Laundar IV, completely brainwashed individuals who had fallen into the AI's cult, who sounded like little more than zombies.

Zarmol didn't have the same manner of speaking, but his talk of the video communique had been coached, that was for sure.

"I understand you're interested in our immortality spore," Zarmol said, getting straight to business and looking between the group. "Yes, it is real, and yes, it works."

Rams laughed. "I've heard of salesmen selling the fountain of youth many a times. Can you prove it?"

Mihael shot Rams a stern look. He'd told them to let him do the talking multiple times. Ayla understood and listened, but Rams, even in her limited experience, seemed to be a brash type. He wouldn't be her first choice for a wingman on diplomatic outings.

Zarmol held up a hand. "No, no. Don't worry. It's a fair question. The answer is yes. We can prove it. In fact, I'd be happy to schedule a facility tour with you. We'll show you how it works on planetary inhabitants and run scans real time to demonstrate our ability to stop cells in the aging process."

"Great. When can we see this?" Mihael asked. "Now?"

Zarmol shook his head. "Unfortunately, security is rather involved. We understand your organization can be a big economic boon for us based on its reach, but we need to get some matters settled first. We're also not ready to export product just yet."

"Why not?" Mihael raised a brow. He looked deflated. He'd been hoping for a payday for this mission, and if the people of the planet delayed him from being able to get the immortality spore, he wouldn't be able to then turn it around for a profit for the pirates. This whole mission could be a bust. Though, from Ayla's perspective, at least she had a little information already. If this planet wasn't ready to export, it gave her time to identify weaknesses and shut down this whole operation.

"Because we're trying to get the populace here one hundred percent acclimated to the spore. We want everyone to be healthy and have longevity before we stretch bigger. It's important for societal stabilization. Even now, we have a faction opposing our new wonder drug, even to the detriment of their own health. Their protests have been unfortunate." He gave a small smile to indicate he was down-playing their impacts.

Ayla perked, very interested in the information of the political landscape of Zenda. She would have to find these opposition leaders and see if she could make contacts. They might be able to help her in her true mission.

"How long do you estimate that'll take? Are we talking weeks? Years?" Mihael sounded desperate. Ayla almost felt bad for the pirate, excepting for the fact he trafficked in illegal goods bad for the Imperium. He could use a little loss.

"We're unsure. Right now, we estimate the population is about sixty to seventy percent acclimated. We're working to enact laws to ensure the population requires the supplement in order to maintain their gainful employment. Economic pressure works best, far better than brute force."

Except in Ayla's mind, economic pressure was brute force. If a man couldn't eat because of the social pressure, it was just as bad or worse than someone grabbing him and strapping him down to force him to inhale the spores. He was backed into a corner. She could already see she stepped into a pressure-filled situation, where even the slightest provocation could make the socio-political climate of the world burst. Zarmol seemed very tense about it, as he should be, but Ayla simply filed the information in the back of her head. She wouldn't act rashly or without a good amount of information. She would wait for the right moment.

"You brought us all the way out here only to deny us?" Mihael sounded incensed, but he kept his expression flat. It was inconsiderate of Zarmol, but given the opportunities involved, the pirates would have little choice but to wait.

"I never promised I would be selling the spores, now did I?" Zarmol said. "I think if you'll go to our communiques, I've been forth-right with you. I'm a salesman, yes, but I'm looking toward the long-term future not a simple quick sale. I'm hoping once you see our facilities and what we can do, we can come to an amicable agreement between my world and your group. Hmm?"

Mihael grumbled his agreement. He didn't have much choice in the matter, but he also didn't have much of a choice if he wanted the benefits of these spores for his people. "When do you think you can set up this meeting for us to tour?"

"Soon," Zarmol said. He snapped his fingers. "I've stored your request in my memory banks. I'll have an answer when I can. But, for now, we can set you up with lodging in the city. You're welcome to explore and get acquainted with our world. The council has set up a very nice place where we are all very happy. We want to encourage tourism."

The pirates looked between each other. Ayla got the sense Mihael had little patience for these stalling tactics. Zarmol wanted them to remain on planet, but why? Regardless, accommodations here had to have been better than the cramped quarters aboard the *Peregrine*.

"Let me discuss my next steps with my crew," Mihael said, leaning back against his seat. "We weren't planning on staying on the planet long and so we'll have to make provisions."

"Of course." Zarmol stood and headed to the bar, where he fraternized with the waitress. The girl paused as if trying to determine if she recognized him, and then she spoke with him fondly. Another odd instance where Ayla noted a problem with people's memories here.

"What do you think?" Mihael asked, breaking Ayla's concentration on the conversation across the room.

"I think we're being set up for something," Rams said, crossing his arms over his chest. "I don't trust him."

"There's something strange about the people here," Ayla said. "There's more than meets the eye with the spore situation, but I don't get the feeling that Zarmol is out to harm us. It's something to do with their chip implants." Ayla touched the side of her cheek where the people from the colony all seemed to have them installed. "It's like a memory bank or something, and it takes a moment for them to process what's going on."

Mihael peered over to the bar, narrowing his eyes. Zarmol inclined his head back to him as if to inquire if he could come back. Mihael held up one finger in response.

"I see the implant," Mihael said. "I've noticed the people here are acting strange, too. Ayla, do you think you can get to the bottom of this so we know what we're dealing with?"

Ayla perked. "Of course. I'll need some leeway to interact with the residents here more. The man at the bar earlier was beginning to trust me." She looked over to where he had sat before, but he was gone now. He'd wanted to court her, but she'd blown off the idea at the time. It could have provided valuable information if she'd been a little more open. But then she'd been instructed to follow Mihael, and she didn't want to push her luck with her newfound job as a pirate.

"If we're going to stay here for a few days, then you might as well," Mihael said.

"You can't seriously be considering wasting more time here," Rams said. "We had an idea, it's bust, come on. This spore nonsense is probably fake anyway. How many eternal life scams have there been over the years? It's the oldest snake oil in the book."

"The boss thinks it's real enough, and if it is, we shouldn't give it up just because we'll be put out for a few days. Let's see what they can offer us. It'll show how serious they are." Mihael raised his hand, and then waved Zarmol back over.

The bald man returned with a fresh drink in his hand. "Have you deliberated?"

"We have, and I think we can stay for a few days until we get a tour. I have seven people in my crew. Do you have enough rooms available?" Mihael asked.

"We have a nice inn right on this street that should be able to accommodate you. It serves two meals a day as well. I apologize for the inconvenience, but I assure you your time spent will be well worth it when you see the product." Zarmol took a sip of his drink. "Shall I show you the way?"

Mihael motioned for Rams to move, and the other pirate slid out of his seat, allowing the captain out of the booth. Ayla stood up on the other side, joining her friends. The captain stood by Zarmol, a few inches taller than the bald man. "Let's go."

8

After they'd gotten settled into their new rooms, Ayla set off into the lobby. Several of the crew were there, chatting with each other by an artificial holographic fire, which provided some heat as well as an aesthetically pleasing visual.

Rams was there, talking with some locals. He looked up, waving to Ayla. "Would you like to join us? We were just about to sit down for the complimentary dinner. Pretty nice place here."

Ayla gave a soft smile to him. "No, I think I'm going to get some fresh air and see if I can't find my way around town. Captain wanted me to get to know the people here and get a sense for their culture and local customs."

"Makes sense. See you a bit later." He returned to talking to the others.

Weaving through the small crowd of people, Ayla made her way to the door, and then outside into the open air. The streets were lit with strips of lights which were strung together across the building tops, pointed downward upon the ground. Small vehicles zoomed through the air.

She hadn't had an idea where she would be headed. Like any major metropolitan area, the cityscape offered vast amounts of potential.

But Ayla didn't want to wander into workspaces or places to shop for trinkets. She wanted to get information on Zenda IV, the government here, the police and military, the state of their society.

Zarmol had mentioned something of a resistance when they were at the bar. If such an insurrectionist entity existed, it would be a good place to start learning about such things, but Ayla also knew better than to start going down a street asking questions about rebels. That's how one found themselves killed or in an interrogation chamber.

She had to make some acquaintances here, which would take time. Potentially more time than they had. Mihael had been itching to get them back off planet, getting the sense this mission was a bust and wouldn't be filling his credit coffers. He was the captain, and at the end of the day, they would follow his lead, but Ayla might have to plan for a contingency where she would stay behind if they decided to go off to more profitable ventures.

There would be at least a few days before the pirate captain became so antsy he'd want to get out of here. The promise of the facility tour gave him some patience, but the patience would wear out at some point.

While lost in her thoughts, a flitter stopped at the end of the current intersection, letting a man out. The flitter had a full window panoramic view, allowing her to see inside. It appeared as if the vehicle was flown via an automated assistant, and it took off without any human passenger inside. The man who stepped out wore a full suit, and Ayla recognized the dark features and brown hair from before, Dorrinal.

Ayla sauntered up the street to greet the man as he watched the flitter take off into the air and back into the skyway. A soft breeze made his hair sway as the flitter accelerated away.

"What brings you back to this section of town?" Ayla asked.

Dorrinal looked at her as if he'd seen her for the first time in her life, and tightened his shoulders as if afraid of a stranger.

Something clicked into him, likely his memory chip activated and recalling their experience. His befuddled expression turned into a soft smile. "Ayla! Great to see you again."

"I thought you didn't recognize me for a second," Ayla teased, stopping in front of him.

"I didn't, I—" He paused and shrugged. "I didn't."

Ayla quirked a brow at him. "That's odd, isn't it? We just met a couple of nights ago."

Dorrinal tapped the memory chip on the side of his cheek. "These aren't perfect. Sometimes, the chip takes a moment to activate and recall the situation."

"Then why get one?" Ayla asked. Perhaps such questioning of societal norms could be dangerous, but Ayla knew this man liked her. It seemed innocuous enough for an outsider to ask such questions. She hoped it wouldn't cause any problems.

"Easy. I had a memory issue to begin with, so this helped me to get myself back to a functioning ability, like it does millions of people across Zenda IV. It actually improves upon basic human memory. Gives me perfect recall of events. Only downside is that small moment."

The talk of his memory issue gave her pause. Was there something about the ecology of this planet that caused memory issues? Or perhaps it was due to the immortality spore itself? If more than fifty percent of the population had taken the spore, and these problems were persistent, then it would make sense that it was some kind of side-effect to their longevity.

"Do you know why you had memory problems from before?" Ayla asked. She tried to sound sweet, hoping her constant questioning wouldn't scare the man away. Dorrinal had seemed too nice so far, and this had been a helpful experiment in learning more about the society here.

Dorrinal shrugged. "No. Must have been born that way or got some condition. Doctors said it's fairly normal for memory loss to occur. Good we have technology, though, to help with these conditions. Yeah?"

"Yeah. Something like that," Ayla said, shifting her eyes away. She wanted to ask about the immortality spore, but she figured she was pressing her luck too much as it was. She had to find a way for it to naturally come up in conversation so Dorrinal wouldn't suspect her of mining him for information. "Where are you headed?"

"I was going downtown to get a bite to eat. Do you want to join me?" His eyes shone hopefully.

"I'd love to," Ayla said, retaining her chipper tone of voice. "Being from off world, I don't know what's good around here. Maybe you can show me something pleasant?"

Her question caused him to perk, and he turned to head down the street around the corner from where Ayla had been before. They came upon a small cafe, and Dorrinal helped himself to a table out front, where they could sit along the street and watch other people pass by and enjoy the warm air as it approached evening time.

Ayla took a seat, scanning over a digital menu embedded into the table. The cafe offered a number of soft stimulants in the form of drinks, as well as flavored protein offerings with local spices. None of the options seemed familiar to Ayla, and so she looked up at Dorrinal. "I'm not sure what I should be getting."

"Right, offworlder." His eyes met hers. "You like it spicy?"

"Not really."

"Sweet?"

"In moderation."

"Hmm..." He scanned the menu again. "Try the white wine reduction glaze on the protein cube. It's just about moderate for everything."

"You've got it." Ayla input her entry on the form, tapping it with her finger. Dorrinal followed by making his own selection. This cafe had bots manning the various stations, with no human personnel in sight. Even back on Terra Prime, small wage jobs had been replaced by bots for the most part, unless it was somewhere nice like the steakhouse Jorus had taken her to in New Austin Megacity. The humanity provided was considered part of the upscale experience. Not that she would complain to her current host about the lack of such amenities.

Eventually, food and drink arrived at the table as Ayla talked to Dorrinal. She gave him the story of how she was a duchess from an agrarian planet she found to be boring, so she sought a life of adventure. He'd seemed to admire her ability to pick up and go jet setting, but he held a job as a research scientist in a local laboratory running quality control processes.

"It's not as exciting as flying from star to star like you, but it pays the bills," Dorrinal said.

"There's nothing wrong with a little stability." Ayla prodded at her protein cube with her fork. The consistency was a little mushy for her tastes, but the flavors weren't offensive. She needed to remind herself she was fortunate to be able to dine at nicer restaurants for the most part. The majority of the population ate like this, and she shouldn't be prissy about it. It fit with her cover story as a duchess, though. "I have a question for you, if you don't mind."

"Of course." His eyes shone brightly at her. He was enamored, which only helped her in this situation.

"Do you know anything about this immortality spore I hear so much about? I came to the planet hearing there's some wonder drug that makes you live forever, and I was wondering if I could get on that train. I don't much like getting older." Ayla smiled softly.

Dorrinal laughed. "Few people do. Yes, I took it. Best decision of my life. I'm about eighty years old, even though I look like I'm thirty-five. In Terra Prime rotations, that is."

"Naturally." Ayla couldn't help but give him a once over. He did have the physique of someone about thirty. Perhaps this spore did perform miracles. On the other hand, he'd referenced his memory issues. They could have had something to do with the spore, they also could have been from another cause entirely, but it seemed too convenient. He'd ingested the spore, had the memory chip, and he was vague about the specifics of his condition. It seemed like a red flag in Ayla's mind.

"I heard there were some people resisting the spore, too." She tried her best to sound casual in the observation.

"Yeah, there's a man named Hervey. He's said to be a lunatic. Something drove him mad. Used to be on track to a seat on the council. But I don't know much." Dorrinal shrugged.

It was about all of the prodding she felt comfortable doing with a stranger. They descended into small talk. His life was as boring as he'd presented it when he said he had a job in the financial markets. He stayed in one place most of the day, living in a cubicle, only getting outside after eight-hour shifts.

Not that Ayla had had it much better as of late in a cramped pirate ship. But at least she'd gotten to travel to different worlds. There was danger involved in her career, but she could handle it.

The sun set into a beautiful red horizon that encompassed the whole of the sky. Ayla looked up, unable to help herself.

"Your hair looks even prettier in this soft glow," Dorrinal said.

"Thank you," Ayla replied, not hesitating to take the compliment. The more he found her attractive, the more she'd be able to get from him information wise.

She finished up her meal, said her goodbyes, and headed back to the residence where their contact had put them up. In her first days on the planet she'd found some good reconnaissance. She could only hope this mission stayed as easy as it had been so far.

9

WHEN SHE RETURNED TO THE PIRATE RESIDENCE, ONLY MIHAEL lingered in the common area. He had a datapad in hand, reading over some material or another, and looked up when the sliding doors opened to allow Ayla to enter. He immediately stood from his position, a stern look on his face. He'd been waiting for her.

Ayla strolled over to him, coming to a stop before the captain. "Good evening, Mihael."

"Where have you been?" he asked.

"You said we should go about the city and try to get a lay of the land, didn't you? So, I did so."

"By yourself."

"Yes, by myself."

Mihael stared at her for a long moment, as if trying to glean something from her soul. He took a step back. "I don't know what it is about you, but I can tell something isn't what it seems. You're too sharp to be some flighty duchess off trying to teach her family a lesson. But all of your records check out. Rams couldn't find anything on you to the contrary."

"Because there's nothing to find," Ayla said, her tone cool and low. She wanted to project confidence, and she'd been in this game long enough to where she didn't get nervous in situations like this. Invariably, in cover missions, someone would question her identity. As a striking woman with red hair, she stood out too much to be completely left alone, but it created a lack of suspicion in her marks at the same time. Men's minds were contradictory at times.

"I believe you. For now. But where did you go? I'd like a full report," Mihael said. He moved over to some of the seating in front of the holographic fire display. He took a seat there, motioning for her to join him.

Ayla followed and helped herself to a seat next to the captain. He could be a little brash, but he worked well as a leader, as a captain. He had a rugged handsomeness to him as well. If she were some runaway duchess, she might be swept away by him, but Ayla had more experience in these matters than the average young runaway.

She told him of her encounter with Dorrinal, the local who'd shown interest with her since she'd gotten here. Technically, her mission for Terra Prime didn't contradict with what the pirates were aiming for on this level either, so she felt comfortable giving him all of the information Dorrinal gave her—the memory issues, that he'd taken the spore, his day-to-day life on this planet, she spared no detail.

Over the course of the conversation, Mihael's features softened. If he had suspected her of any duplicity when she'd arrived, he didn't seem to harbor any ill-feelings now. He ran a hand back through his hair. "That is the most detailed report anyone's ever given me." He chuckled to himself. "I need to get more people in the crew like you."

"I thought you were just saying you didn't trust me?" Ayla gave him a soft smile.

"We're pirates. I don't trust anyone," Mihael said. "But I appreciate your reconnaissance work. If you can find out more about this spore, I think it'd be a big help to us."

Ayla noted two patrons in the corner talking to each other. One had a transparent rubber mask attached to a cylinder. He depressed a button on the cylinder, which filled the mask with what appeared to be some mist or powder. The man breathed in deeply while the woman beside him eagerly watched. He held his breath for about ten seconds before exhaling again and removing his face from the mask.

"That's it?" he asked.

"That's it," the woman beside him said.

The man leaned in, giving the woman a firm embrace before kissing her on the lips. He pulled back halfway, a grin crossing his face. "Perfect. I'm immortal like you now."

"We can be together forever," the woman said.

Mihael had been talking to Ayla, but she'd stopped paying attention. "...which I found during our last mission to the traders' outpost on Dinbar V. Are you listening to me?" He blinked.

"Ah, sorry," Ayla said, motioning her head toward the couple in the doorway. "You said you wanted to find out more information about the spore. I think I just witnessed someone taking the substance."

Mihael looked back over his shoulder to eye the couple. They seemed to be in their reverie still, enjoying each other's company and not seeing much else of the world. They didn't have to be incognito in observing them as a consequence.

One thing Ayla had learned from both Dorrinal and witnessing these two is that this world seemed to have no secrecy behind the spore. People took it openly and spoke of it as if it were a matter of brushing their teeth in the morning. It made it easy for her to glean information, though she still had to be careful about prying too hard into the memory issues associated with it. Ayla noted the man did not have the memory implant over his cheek, while the woman did have hers. It further confirmed her suspicion that the memory loss was related to the spore somehow.

"Let's get going to dinner, then," the woman said to her beau.

The man pulled back from her turning to leave, and then paused. "Where were we going again?"

The woman cocked her head. "You said you had reservations."

"I did?" The man cocked his head in confusion.

"You did."

"Well, I can't for the life of me remember."

"Hold on." The woman narrowed her eyes, which might have been her trying to retrieve the memories from her chip. "It doesn't look like you told me any specifics about where we were supposed to go, but you certainly told me you made reservations for this evening to celebrate."

"It must have been somewhere nice if that's the case," the man said. He didn't seem to correlate what just happened with ingesting the spore with any memory problems. Neither did the woman. Did these memory chips manipulate people so they couldn't come to the conclusion? It sounded insidious, much like the brainwashing OVER-MIND had done to the inhabitants Ayla had seen on Laundar IV but on a much subtler level.

The two stepped outside the room and continued their conversation. If anything, this was the confirmation Ayla needed to understand the spore had terrible side-effects. They'd gone unmentioned by anyone on the planet she'd encountered.

"Did you catch all of that?" Ayla asked, centering her attention back on Mihael.

The captain shook his head. He faced the wrong direction in comparison to her, able to sneak glances, but he hadn't focused on the conversation as she had.

"He's got confirmed memory loss. And it seemed to be in line with the timing of when he ingested the spore. I think there's more than meets the eye to this proposed immortality. There are side-effects."

"It's like that with almost all drugs." Mihael frowned. "No matter how doctors try to manipulate the human body, there's always a drawback to tampering with nature."

"What are we going to do about it?" Ayla asked.

The captain's forehead wrinkled as he went quiet with thought. "Nothing yet. We're going to gather more information on what's going on with the production on this planet and see if we can't make a profit out of it anyway. If it causes memory loss and people are stupid, it's not my problem."

Ayla opened her mouth to protest. Unlike the pirate, she had a sense of duty toward her fellow humans. As an imperial agent, she had to protect the common citizens from nefarious drugs being propagated across systems. She couldn't allow it to happen, now more than ever with the dangers involved. She could only imagine a populace across worlds that couldn't remember what they had for breakfast. Many people had such short attention spans as it was. It would be a nightmare.

"What are you thinking?" Mihael asked.

"I don't like it," Ayla said. Even though she had to follow his lead and keep his trust for the mission, she didn't want to outright lie as much as she could manage it.

"You'll learn fast if you want to make a living in this business, you're going to have to check your morals at the door. What we're doing is already illegal, exporting some unknown substance to different imperial systems. So what if it's got some drawbacks? I've moved any number of scheduled or illicit substances. This is no different, it just has the promise of being more profitable than anything I've touched in my entire life."

"But it can hurt people. It's going to hurt people. Can you imagine the effects if this ripples across the entire Imperium?" Ayla shook her head. "It could devastate all of humanity. There has to be some line you won't cross."

Mihael chuckled. "You really are an innocent princess. We'll clear you of any of your ignorant ideas soon enough. The galaxy's not a nice place. It's not like your sheltered little home castles."

Ayla crossed her arms over her chest, trying to look indignant. If only he knew the reality of everything she'd seen. But she had to keep her cover. "I think I want to go to my room and think about all this."

"Don't think too hard. You'll only upset yourself. It's why a lot of us pirates drown ourselves in drink." Mihael stood, motioning toward the bar before he headed that direction.

10

AYLA SETTLED INTO HER ROOM AND SPENT A GOOD HOUR READING ALL the information she could about the planet before turning out the lights and letting her head hit the pillow. It had been a fairly long day learning as much as she could about the Zendan population. What she'd found troubled her.

The populace appeared to be mostly docile and stable, but not in a healthy manner. They were almost too passive in their acceptance of the ordinances that came down from the council, a corporate ruling body which controlled the planet. Being off the Imperial radar for so long, the council acted with complete autonomy and no oversight.

Even though there was mention of a resistance brewing from their contact Zarmol, she found no mention of it in the local news sources, ethernet rumors, nor anyone talking about it in casual conversation among the populace. It was like the resistance didn't exist. She couldn't even find any information on the man Hervey who Dorrinal told her was involved with the group.

But the resistance did exist, or it wouldn't have been mentioned. She still had no good leads on how to find it. It didn't matter, she would have plenty of time to do more research the next day, and maybe even the day after that if their contacts remained slow and didn't schedule their inspections of their facilities in a timely manner. All of this was so strange. There was a piece missing to whatever was going on with this spore situation, but Ayla couldn't determine what with the information she had.

She closed her eyes, letting darkness overcome her. Then, something clicked in her room. Her eyes popped open, but the lights weren't on. She couldn't tell what was going on. Was it Mihael coming back drunk and thinking he could take advantage of her? The captain had shown he'd had a predilection toward too much of the sauce. She couldn't see him as the type who would cause her problems, however. Despite his piracy and his other flaws, he seemed a decent man.

Someone moved within the room. Multiple someones. Ayla sat up to see several shadows in motion, flanking either side of the bed to make sure she had nowhere to run.

Ayla scooted out from under the covers. She only wore a small, thin nightgown, which rode up far too high on her legs for her liking in a situation like this. She didn't have time to stand before the shadows fell upon her. They were men, their faces concealed with dark masks. These weren't her pirate friends.

"Gag her so she can't scream," one of the men said in a low tone.

Before she could react, the men had her arms, and someone placed something over her head. She tried to yell, but the sound died under the cloth they'd placed over her. Ayla kicked at one of their heads, connecting with hard contact, making him stumble back against the wall, crashing. She was certain they didn't want to make noise, but she would make as much as she possibly could so they might get caught in the act. Whoever these people were would have to deal with her pirate friends and security soon enough.

She brought her legs up like a scissor around a man's torso, turning over and flipping him off to the side as well. She was free of the men who grabbed her for now. Before the hood obscured her view and cut off her ability to yell for help, she thought she'd counted four of them in total. Ayla reached up to try to get the cloth off her face, but the opening had scrunched around her neck, making it difficult to pull off. Her attackers weren't incompetent.

More arms grabbed her, ripping her arms away from the hood at her neck. She'd have to keep fighting this blind. She kicked at these men once more, but they'd grown wise to her only means of defense. Others secured her legs so she wouldn't move. She was no match for four men, even with her genetic enhancements, which gave her better than average speed and strength. They'd caught her flat-footed, asleep, and she had been utterly surprised by the idea of someone attacking her. She'd had no warning whatsoever.

They'd planned well enough. She couldn't run, she couldn't maneuver, and with the cloth over her head, she couldn't even scream effectively.

If these men wanted her dead, though, they could have killed her very easily. Logic dictated they wanted her alive. But for what purpose? She tried to think of all of the situations she'd been in. Her contact, Zarmol, hadn't seemed particularly interested in her. Could Dorrinal be a part of this group? He had been very persistent. Or perhaps the couple she'd observed taking the immortality spore in the common area? Someone else entirely?

Ayla would have liked to have thought she'd have noticed anyone observing her as an outsider. She was a trained agent, after all, but she couldn't help but have the sneaking suspicion she'd overlooked something in her visit to Zenda. Perhaps the political situation here was more precarious than she had realized.

Deciding it best to conserve her energy, Ayla went limp. She allowed the men to grab her and hold her down. They whispered to each other, something she couldn't make out, and then the room went quiet without so much as a rustle.

Were they going to carry her out of here? Her answer came in the form of a swift knock to the head, which sent her swirling into darkness.

11

AYLA AWOKE IN A WHITE ROOM WITH METAL CABINETS AND MACHINERY all around her. Whoever had taken her had strapped her down onto a table in a very uncomfortable position, to where she could hardly move her head to get a view around her. The straps were made of metal, too, bonds she wouldn't be able to break without considerable assistance.

She counted herself lucky that she didn't sleep in the nude or something equally inappropriate. She liked comfortable shorts and a soft tank top. Although it still showed more skin than she typically would have liked to have flaunted in public, at least whenever she encountered her captors, she wouldn't feel too embarrassed.

Even though she could hardly get a decent view of the place from her position on her back, with bright lights shining down on her face, she could crane her neck enough to see she had been taken to some kind of laboratory. It was modern, which told her Zenda at least kept up with importing advancements from the Imperium, with holographic displays and instruments appearing to be technical in nature. The room had no other table other than the one she was strapped to. She couldn't spot a door, but it might have been on the wall toward where her head faced.

The sound of an electronic automatic slider confirmed her suspicion as to the room's exit a moment later, and a shadow fell upon her.

When her eyes adjusted to the figure blocking the light above her, she made out dark features of a man she'd not expected to see. "Dorrinal?" Ayla asked, recognizing the man she'd just encountered.

He'd told her he worked as a scientist in a lab. Quality control. A chill ran down her spine as she considered what he might have meant by those words. What if he'd meant *population control* but in a polite way? He hadn't sounded like he'd been doing anything nefarious with his work, but one could hardly tell the extent of someone's inner demons based on flirting small talk at a dinner table. What had she gotten herself into?

"Pardon, do I know you?" Dorrinal asked, but then he cocked his head in the awkward tic where several of Zenda's residents activated their memory chips. "Oh. Ayla? What are you doing here?"

"That's the question I wanted to ask. What *am* I doing here?" She tugged at her restraints so they would make some noise and hopefully get his attention and sympathy. He didn't seem to have been a part of the group who brought her here. Maybe he would release her.

Dorrinal stared at the restraints with a frown. He seemed confused by the situation. "I was told I was going to be helping with a patient who'd had a failed immortality spore inhalation. Sometimes, there's user error in these processes. The canister shoots the spore into the air, and it has to be breathed in rapidly and in sufficient quantities or it doesn't have an impact. But you're an offworlder, aren't you? Why would you be getting the spore?"

"I didn't intend on getting it," Ayla said. "Someone brought me from where I was staying. I don't know what's going on."

"I'm going to go call my supervisor and find out," Dorrinal said, spinning. His lab coat brushed against the top of Ayla's head.

A supervisor wouldn't help. The person would probably convince Dorrinal to force the immortality spore into her, saddling her with the same memory problems as the people of the colony. She couldn't let that happen. "No, don't call anyone. I'm glad you're here."

Dorrinal stopped in his tracks as the door automatically opened for him again. "Why shouldn't I call anyone?"

Footsteps sounded in the hall beyond. This was a bigger facility than merely this office. Ayla still couldn't figure out exactly where she was at. A simple office, or was this place somewhere with more importance? Whoever had kidnapped her obviously hadn't liked her gathering information on the colony.

It had all gone too easily until this point. Her questioning of locals like Dorrinal, her observations of people taking the spore. She'd gotten complacent and not been discreet enough. Thinking back to her conversations, though, she hadn't noticed anyone observing her. Even when she was lax in the way she handled conversations, she surely had enough training to have noticed anyone spying on her or placing a bug within sight. And her conversations had been in mostly random places. They couldn't have had listening devices there in advance, unless...

Her eyes widened as it dawned upon her. The memory chips. They could be accessed by people outside of the person where they'd been installed. Of course. She'd garnered suspicion of the local government, and they cross-referenced the data with the chips.

The immortality spore and its side-effects now seemed much more insidious to Ayla. The memory loss was being used by the council here to control the populace, their memories, to survey them. All of this represented illegal invasions of privacy under Imperium law, but Ayla had to find a way to prove it for her reports.

Before that, she had to find a way to get out of here and survive without being turned into some memoryless drone member of their population.

"Because..." Ayla said slowly, trying to come up with a good reason he should listen to her and not his own instincts to go to a superior. "It's me. You remember. This has to be some kind of mistake. Yes, a mistaken identity. You know, I was supposed to have a tour of the facility. If you let me out of my restraints, I can go find the tour group I was supposed to meet, and we can clear up this misunderstanding."

Dorrinal eyed her with consideration. Even though they'd spent some time together, he barely knew her, and it was a big ask for him to trust her right now. She had to rely on the fact he had some attraction to her from the start. He moved over to the side of the table, depressing a button releasing the clamps on her wrists and feet.

Ayla sat up on the table, stretching her arms out, and then cracking her neck. "Thank you. That was about the most uncomfortable place I'd laid down in years."

There wasn't much to do to conceive of a plan. She had to find her way around this place before she determined what to do next—and figure out exactly who was responsible for kidnapping her and bringing her here to begin with. Dorrinal knew nothing, and even if he had some information, his memory chip likely would have controlled what he would be able to impart.

She slipped off the table and onto her feet, standing in front of Dorrinal, her eyes coming up to about his mouth. He looked down at her.

"Where are you going?" he asked.

"To figure out who brought me here and see if I can't rectify some mistakes. I think it'd be easier for everyone if you just forgot you'd seen me here, yeah?" Ayla tried to make her eyes as big as possible. Hopefully, he would find some sympathy.

Dorrinal brought his hand back to his head, scratching just behind his ear with nervousness. "I guess so. I wouldn't want to cause you any more trouble. We can meet up again, when everything gets settled?" He eyed her hopefully.

"Of course. Wouldn't miss it for the world." Ayla gave him a soft pat on the arm before sidestepping him toward the door. It opened once more with the automatic hiss, revealing a hallway giving her two options of directions to go. Both looked like they continued on for a long way. This was a big complex, one more piece of information. It might have been the processing center for the immortality spore. Perhaps this kidnapping had been a blessing in disguise.

Before she could get drawn back into conversation with Dorrinal, Ayla made a quick decision of which way to go. She turned left and headed out of the lab into the corridor.

12

AYLA TRIED TO WALK WITH CONFIDENCE AS SHE PASSED SEVERAL OTHER people on her way through the facility. This was a busy place, whatever the function of this building, with people working, moving about, and talking with each other in the hallways. It was also a rather large building with far too many options for directions.

A couple of men in lab coats passed by. No one appeared to be looking for her nor sounding any security alert. She could probably risk a casual confrontation with some of the people here.

"Excuse me," Ayla asked, pausing in her step.

The two men turned around to note her. "Yes?" one of them asked.

"I'm new and lost. I was supposed to meet my supervisor in the production facility," Ayla said, making up a quick story. It seemed something reasonable a new intern might ask. "Do you know where I might find it?"

The man who had answered the first time cocked his head, and then pointed down the corridor. "There's a lift at the end of the hall where you're headed. Take it down two levels, head out to the right. You'll get to a big loading door you can't miss. The chemical production plant is in there. If it's not open, there's a smaller entrance further down on the same wall."

Ayla brandished her best sheepish smile. "Thank you so much."

"No problem."

She continued forward, not looking back. As much as the man had been helpful, she didn't want to press her luck and get him speculating as to whether she belonged there or not. So far, she'd managed to evade entanglements that would cause her any problems.

Before she arrived at the lift, she spotted a door labeled "storage closet." Ayla looked down at herself and realized she'd been more than lucky the men hadn't questioned her attire. Even though she had covered herself well enough, she still didn't have appropriate attire for a business environment, let alone a scientific research facility.

This door didn't have an automatic opener, so Ayla turned the handle and pressed the door inward. Inside were shelves with piles of what appeared to be cleaning supplies. She also spotted a lab coat and goggles. It would do nicely.

She grabbed the lab coat, which was slightly too big for her lithe frame, and also the goggles, which she placed over her face. She then took her hair and knotted it, tying it into a ponytail. It wasn't the best disguise, but she had to think that other than Dorrinal, the people here wouldn't be recalling her features.

Feeling better dressed for the part of someone who worked here, Ayla closed the door and headed into the lift. She hit the controls to go to the first level and descended as the gears clicked with mechanical noises.

The lift arrived, opening to allow Ayla exit. She followed the directions the man had given her, and sure enough she saw a large opening she believed must have been the loading doors. Inside was a large warehouse-style room about two stories tall, with dozens of processing machines inside. It gave off an odor of dust and chemicals. Some machines appeared to be for grinding the spores, others for manufacturing dispenser devices, and a conveyor for assembling the cartridges. At the end of the conveyor, robots placed the product into boxes for distribution.

Even though it was a large facility, if this was what they had to service this entire planet, Ayla could see why Zarmol had told them they weren't ready for exporting.

She wished she had her visor on her instead of these safety goggles. The visor had a fashionable outward appearance, but it also acted as a mobile interface allowing her to take video and pictures of the facility. It would have been nice to have for both the pirates and her imperial mission. But all she had was her own two eyes. She tried to take in as much as she could as she approached the doors, looking for weak points where she might be able to exploit if she needed to come in here and destroy the facility.

There was a spot upon a power pack wall Ayla spotted immediately upon entering where, if one were to place an explosive, it would be able to exponentially compound a blast. Useful.

Dozens of people worked in the large facility alongside the machinery, computer readings, and robotics. None seemed to notice her at first, allowing Ayla to walk around and inspect some of the machinery. It was a clean manufacturing facility, standard to other pharmaceutical plants she'd encountered in her time. As an agent of the Imperium, she'd had to raid such facilities on more than one occasion. Far too many people tended to abuse drugs when given the opportunity, whether through money laundering, stealing, or selling illicit substances.

She weaved through the large room with machinery scattered throughout. When she passed part of the production line, she caught sight of Zarmol, the council representative who'd met with them at the pub when they'd first arrived. He hadn't spotted her yet, but Ayla froze, and then backpedaled so she could put herself partially into cover. If he recognized her, it could be trouble.

As she considered her kidnapping, it could have been him who ordered her brought here in the first place. Dorrinal seemed to have no idea what was going on, a low-level technician, but Zarmol would have been the type to have been kept abreast of intelligence operations on the planet. Anger rose within Ayla, but she had to keep her cool and not act rashly.

Alongside Zarmol stood a strange looking figure, taller than all of the other humans by a full head, lankier as well, and completely contained within a brown environment suit. The suit had a green glow from the front of it, and the head was box-shaped with smooth corners, an odd design. The helmet exhausted some gas, which fizzled up above its head whenever the person breathed.

Why would someone be in an environment suit here? It perplexed Ayla. Perhaps it was someone being careful with the fumes these produced. Ayla wondered if she might have accidentally been inhaling these spores that could give her lasting side-effects. She certainly hoped not. But the suit could also be used to conceal someone's identity. If there were seedy operations going on here, it would have made sense for them to do so.

"As you can see," Zarmol said, motioning to the machinery in the room, "our production facility is at full capacity. We're in the process of building three more just like this to upgrade our rate of production, but it will be a few months before those are operational. With this one alone, however, I have no doubt we'll be able to capture the entirety of this planet on schedule."

He didn't seem to notice Ayla, and she did her best to stay out of his direct line of sight. The way Zarmol spoke sounded like how a subordinate would be speaking to a manager in for an inspection visit. But who was this fellow in the mask? He had such an odd body shape, which bothered Ayla, but she couldn't quite place why.

"Very good," the suited man replied in a voice-modulated tone, which seemed to emanate from the suit rather than the person beneath it. More curious. He went to extreme lengths to hide his identity.

Ayla wished she had her visor on her, or some of her other gear. This was the type of conversation that merited recording, and now she wouldn't have any evidence beyond what her memory provided. Still, she could listen and learn and catch any wrongdoers later.

"Do you think you'll be able to get one hundred percent of the population to agree to taking the spore?" the suited man asked.

"So far, most of the population has been willing. We've been running propaganda commercials about health deterioration and aging that have been very effective. Our ministry of information has also been removing harmful messaging about the spore from the ethernet citing misinformation campaigns. Most people have gone very willingly, with a good portion agreeing to take the spore because of social pressure.

"As a greater amount of the population has it, we'll be able to enact small changes to our society where those who don't have the spore aren't able to receive medical treatment. After all, why spend time treating those who would die anyway? And then, with the memory implant chip, we'll be able to use that to direct the flow of commerce so no one without one can use credits on planet. It will weed out the rest."

"A viable strategy, but you still won't get a hundred percent through such measures," the suited man replied. "It's hardly possible to get humans to agree on anything. There will always be those who rebel for the sake of rebelling. How are your insurrectionists, anyway?"

"We've yet to be able to isolate and purge them. Give it time," Zarmol said.

Imperial law dictated a governing body had the right to quell riots or protests that were out of hand. But she hadn't seen anything of the sort since she'd arrived here. Granted, it had only been a few days and this rebelling group may well be planning action, but it seemed like there weren't any laws being violated. If these people simply had differing opinions on the spore, they were due the same protection as imperial subjects as anyone else. The planetary security forces would be the aggressors, if they instigated the fights. This could get messy, legally, if it continued the way it sounded like it was going to.

"We will need one hundred percent compliance in order to ensure phase two of our plan goes well, and the enslavement of the population can begin," the suited man said. Even though the voice came through a changer within the suit, he sounded so cold and calculating it sent a shiver down Ayla's spine.

Zarmol seemed to have a similar fear of the suited man, tense in all of his body language, looking up out of the corner of his eye as if the suited man could lash out at him at any moment. "Of course. We are doing everything we can to ensure we proceed on schedule for your plans."

"You will get rewarded when the time comes. You've seen the vast stores of resources we can offer your planet. Anything the Terran Imperium can offer pales in comparison."

Who were these people? How could they make such wild claims? Ayla hadn't heard of any kind of uprising that had greater resources than the seat of the Imperium. No world outside of Terra Prime had even close to the capital accumulated on humanity's home planet.

This was a conspiracy far beyond what she had expected to find, and it meant it could span worlds. There might be a true insurrection brewing, but among whom? Local governors on the fringes of the Imperium sometimes held delusions of grandeur, much like the one she had met on Laundar IV, but they had posed no bigger threat than a minor outpost causing trouble.

To fight the Imperium, the space Marines, the entire star navy, would take greater than half the aristocracy. Could such a conspiracy run so deep without someone in the agency having found out about it?

Before Ayla could think of the answers, the suited man and Zarmol moved her way. She had to vacate her position of cover and hide before she could be spotted. She turned around and began walking, trying to become as inconspicuous as possible, before spotting a small communications room in the corner of this giant facility. It had an ansible crystal, which would allow interstellar communication. It was past time she summoned some bigger guns. This conspiracy she'd uncovered was too big for her to handle alone.

She hurried for the room and closed the door behind her to get out of the line of sight of Zarmol, hoping she hadn't been spotted.

13

———

USING A COMMUNICATIONS CENTER IN AN ENEMY STRONGHOLD WASN'T the safest of ideas, but Ayla had weighed her situation against the risk before entering the room. One, she needed a quick place to hide away from the tall man in the environment suit and Zarmol. Two, there was no guarantee she wouldn't get captured and kidnapped again before she could find a different mode of communications off world. Three, even if she returned to the pirates, it wasn't as if calling from their facilities would be safer for her—it would only out her as an agent to the people she'd been in deep cover with.

It would be better to impart the information. That way if something were to happen to her, the agency would know what she knew, and they would be able to send reinforcements to do something.

She booted up the terminal inside the room, a standard ansible communications array, and input the proper frequencies to open a line with Terra Prime. Then, she input the private sub-frequency enabling her to get into contact with the agency. Fortunately, she had the numbers memorized for situations like this where she'd have to get in contact in a pinch.

Ayla took a seat on a swivel chair, waiting for the terminal to do its work.

The ansible crystal glowed as it connected to the galactic network, sending a signal through folds in space that enabled communication. The crystals were expensive to attain. Not everyone could afford one. Only major corporations and members of the aristocracy. Most of the crystals were hoarded by the imperial navy, ensuring each of their larger vessels had such communications capability.

Audio came up on the line. "Who is this? Do you have the right frequency? Do you know what time it is?" The voice sounded groggy and not too happy to be receiving a call, but it was the familiar gravelly voice of Jorus, her handler.

"Jorus, it's me, Ayla," Ayla said, relaxing her shoulders in instant relief at being able to communicate with her superior. It had been too long, not having been in contact with him to be able to deliver a report since before she was on the starliner over to the pirates' asteroid base.

"You of all people should know better than to call me this early. Why—"

"I don't have much of a choice. I'm on the planet Zenda. It's a world on the outer reaches of the Imperium where our agents haven't visited in a millennium."

"I haven't heard of it."

"No doubt. It's nice to hear a friendly voice, I have to say." Ayla pursed her lips. It was a huge relief not to have to speak to someone deceptively, to pretend to be someone she wasn't.

"Good enough to head with me to Proxima Centauri? I hear their spatio-golf along their skyline is to die for. Beautiful lights of greens and blues as you travel along the grav platforms. You're due for a vacation, you know."

Ayla chuckled. "We'll see. I don't have time for that now. I'm in some facility where they produce a spore which, in theory, grants a person immortality. It seems your sources were right."

"Good find. Are you destroying the place?"

"I will be. But there's more to it. There's a plot to enslave this entire planet. The spores have some kind of side-effect where a person loses their capacity for long-term memory. The inhabitants are given a memory chip implant to stave off the effects, and the board govern-ment here both has access to said memories for surveillance and to manipulate them. They're planning on getting everyone here on the spore in order to create some sort of slave population. It sounds like there's a big insurrection or overthrow of the Imperium brewing. Have you heard of anything big on the home front?"

"Can't say I have. I doubt anyone has the capability to pull off such a scheme. Do you have a name or a face by chance to go along with this plot? I could run it through the database."

"No, just one of the locals. There's a very tall man in an environ-mental suit he's meeting with, no doubt to keep his identity hidden. I'll need to get more information. But I think I'll also need help. This plot is something bigger than I can chew."

"I'll see if I can't send a team of space Marines to assist you. They might be a couple of weeks out because of travel, though. Where did you say you were again?" Jorus asked.

"Zenda."

The sound of tapping came through the ansible as Jorus inputted the name. "That world's coming up uninhabited."

"I told you the Imperium hadn't been here in a long time. Our databanks are mistaken. Something we should correct immediately. It also begs the question as to whether there are more worlds like this out here."

"I'm sure there are. The galaxy is a vast place, and our records are murky from the era of three emperors and before. It's our duty to ensure nothing like that ever happens to our civilization again."

Ayla barely stopped herself from rolling her eyes. "You don't have to give me the pitch. I'm on board with serving the Imperium. Just take note in case something happens to me. I've been kidnapped here once already, and I get the feeling I'm not safe going forward. I—"

The door the communication room opened. Ayla turned immedi-ately to see who was there.

"Ayla? You cut off."

"I'm afraid she won't be able to answer you," a man said, Zarmol, who stood there with a blaster pistol in his hand, pointed straight at

Ayla. "I think we've had enough fun for the day. Computer, end transmission."

Ayla scrambled to her feet, but there was no way she would be able to get past the man. She'd trapped herself in the room with no exit save for straight through him. And she didn't have any weapons to counter his.

14

EVEN THOUGH THE FIGHT SEEMED FUTILE, AYLA CHARGED AT ZARMOL.

His blaster discharged right at the moment she stepped forward, narrowly missing and hitting the communications console behind her. The machine sparked, giving Ayla an opening to jam the base of her palm into the man's jaw.

He stumbled backward, hitting the doorframe before using it to stabilize himself and lift his weapon again. "Security is on the way. This is a completely futile fight. You can't get past us all."

"I'm not going to let you take me lying down," Ayla said. She knew he was right, which was never a good place to be. One had to have confidence that there was at least a chance to win and, for that, she'd need to get his blaster pistol out of his hand and secure it herself.

She delivered a kick to his wrist to try to knock it free, succeeding in loosening his grip on the pistol. He dropped the weapon, which clanked on the floor. She scrambled to pick it back up, but he kicked at her side, resulting in a hard blow to her ribs, forcing her to fall over into the communications terminal.

There wasn't enough room to maneuver for a proper fight. Not that she'd have much of a shot against a bigger man facing him head-on. The only hope she'd have would be to get the weapon and find her way out into the big open room where she could use the machinery for cover. Hopefully, there, she could find some kind of way to escape.

One step at a time.

Unfortunately, Zarmol didn't seem to be letting up on her. He pressed forward, kicking at her again. It was all Ayla could do to lift her hands and block the boot coming her way, which hurt her arms on the receiving end of it. It was better than letting her ribs get hit again. A few more kicks like that, and he'd bruise or break them for sure.

Being on the defensive and off her feet didn't help matters. Zarmol kept kicking her repeatedly until her arms fell, and he was able to strike another hard boot to her body. This time, Ayla rolled out of the way, close to the weapon laying on the ground. She reached out to it, but Zarmol stamped down on her hand before she could reach it.

Her hand throbbed in pain, and Ayla let out a yelp. The more she fought, the more she'd end up crippled.

Zarmol kept his foot on her hand, grinding it against the floor with the toe of his boot. "Stop. Resisting. If you knew what's good for you, you'd let it happen. I'm doing you a favor, you know. I'm letting you become one of the first offworlders to have a chance at eternal life. Isn't that thrilling? You can live forever just like the rest of my people here. No more getting old, no more withering and decaying. You'll be happy."

"You'll steal my memories," Ayla said through clenched teeth, the pain flaring as she tried to pull her hand away. His weight on her proved too much, however. Her arm went limp as she finally gave out from the strain.

"That I will. I wish you hadn't made any kind of communication. But it's not going to matter. We're going to have a whole world under our control. They'll think what we tell them to think. Remember what we tell them to remember. Everything you did is completely futile."

"I made a difference. Even if I die."

Zarmol laughed. "I wouldn't do something so inhumane. I already told you you're going to be living forever. But enough chatting. You've been too much of a thorn in our sides already. We'll get you processed, and then the rest of your little pirate crew along the way."

He drew his foot back again, but Ayla was in no position to grab the gun anymore. Her hand hurt so bad she couldn't clench her fingers. Tears streaked down her face from the pain. This wasn't the type of fight she'd ever wanted to be in, one of brute force in closed quarters, but she had at least succeeded in contacting Jorus.

Whether Zarmol knew it or not, his days were numbered, and so was the council and whoever else was conspiring here to enslave a population. The Imperium would win, and she could rest easy knowing she did her job. Sacrificing herself with valor wouldn't bother her in the least.

The thoughts did her no good though as he delivered a hard kick directly to her face. This time, she had no way to shield herself, and she went from seeing stars to seeing blackness.

15

SHE AWOKE BACK IN THE LAB, CLAMPED TO THE SAME TABLE SHE HAD been in before. Dorrinal stood over a counter, preparing a dose of the spores in a dispenser. Zarmol stood beside him, hands on his hips, waiting and grimacing with impatience.

Ayla tugged at her restraints, realizing there wouldn't be an easy escape this time. She had talked Dorrinal into letting her go before, but it wouldn't work again, not with Zarmol here to witness.

"Dorrinal, please," she pleaded anyway. She had to try and, fortunately, Zarmol hadn't gagged her. He'd probably intended for her to be sedated through the procedure, but she'd woken up just in time to see the immortality spore lock into the dispenser with a *click*. In a few moments, it would be sprayed in her face, and she would lose her memories much like everyone on the colony had who had ingested this spore.

Dorrinal looked back. "How do you know my name?"

"Never mind her," Zarmol said. "She is an enemy agent trying to manipulate you with falsehoods. Continue with the procedure."

Ayla's eyes widened. Dorrinal didn't remember her. He had just seen her about an hour beforehand, they'd gone out together, and yet nothing. This was another manipulation due to the memory chip, this time on a deep personal level. What an insidious plot. The spore lulls people into a sense of safety, and then they can have all of what they remember removed. Rebellious thoughts, favorability of leaders, it all could be gone.

But the people would achieve near immortality. The side-effects cut like a razor's edge.

She pushed against her restraints once more. "Dorrinal, you know me. We've spent time together. We went to a restaurant together. You showed me the local cuisine. Try to remember!"

"It's all lies," Zarmol spat. "This is why we must inject her with the spores. She needs to become one of us. Her offworlder tendencies are destructive to our society. She can't be allowed to continue without understanding what it's like to have a long view of society, one where it has to be sustainable. She needs to see." He pointed toward her. "Release the spores."

Dorrinal paused. He had confusion in his eyes. Part of him seemed to believe her, but he also worked here and was loyal to his people. "Why would she make up knowing me?" He tapped against his memory chip with his free hand. "How come I don't remember this? My chip might be malfunctioning." His eyes went into a state of panic. "I need to see a tech immediately."

"You need to do your job," Zarmol said. "This is for the board and for all of Zenda. Like I said, she's an offworlder who's manipulating you."

"Then why would we be granting her our greatest gift?" Dorrinal cocked his head.

Ayla had succeeded in removing some of the trust Dorrinal had for his superior. If she could push further, make him sense there was something more wrong here... "I don't want the spore, Dorrinal. They're trying to force it on me. Please, let me go!"

Zarmol's face reddened, and his fist clenched. Then, he swiped at Dorrinal and the dispenser, taking the device from his hands. "I'm sorry, Dr. Dorrinal, but I need to do this myself if you're not able to perform your function. Leave the room and leave this to me. The board will contact you when your services are needed."

Dorrinal's brow wrinkled as he looked between Zarmol and Ayla. This situation clearly didn't sit right with him, but what could he do. He nodded to his superior. "Okay, sir. I'll be outside. I still don't understand what's going on here."

"You will. We'll brief you later," Zarmol said.

It appeared to be enough for the doctor. He stepped toward the door, and then outside, leaving Ayla alone with Zarmol.

The older man breathed out a heavy sigh through his nose, turning to Ayla. "Why do you have to make this so complicated? We could have had you injected and installed with a chip with no problem, but you persist in causing us trouble."

"Because what you're doing is wrong," Ayla said.

Zarmol laughed. "Says the pirate."

Ayla narrowed her eyes. She was no pirate, and he probably knew her true identity at this point if he checked the ansible logs, but she wasn't about to break character and totally blow her cover because he egged her on. If the man looked for confirmation as to her agent status, she wouldn't give him the satisfaction of tricking it out of her.

"We have a code of honor," Ayla said instead. "People have choice, free will. That's what the Robeni pirates are about. The ability to go out and do what you want, when you want. If you steal memories, then you're just a tyrant."

"A tyrant, maybe, but one who is looking for the long-term health of our planet," Zarmol said.

"Which is why you're selling out a population as slaves?" Ayla had him this time. Maybe she could prod him to learn more.

Zarmol tensed. "You heard. No matter. You won't remember soon enough. You see, it still is for the long-term good of my people. When individuals think for themselves, that's when danger occurs. Too many wills pulling against one another until finally it breaks. We've seen it so many times over history. This way, we're removing a certain amount of wills from the equation. Including yours. You won't be able to harm what we're doing here, nor the profit we're going to gain from it."

Ayla perked despite being restrained. So, it *was* a profit motive controlling Zarmol. She wondered what the suited man had promised him. Fortune? No, he probably already had a good amount of wealth amassed in his position. It must have been power.

"And you'll be the petty tyrant imposing your will, hmm?"

"Call it what you must, but everyone will be better off for it. Now, we're done talking. And you're done being a nuisance." He stepped toward her, adjusting his grip on the spore dispenser. She would have mere moments before the substance entered her system.

The idea of losing her memories instilled more fear in her than she'd ever experienced. Ayla struggled against her restraints, squirming, pushing, doing everything she could to break from them. Her muscles ached when she pressed her wrists upward, trying to get the restraints to break, but to no avail. She was trapped there. Nothing would be able to save her from what Zarmol meant to impose upon her.

The restraints had no give. This would be the end of her. If she couldn't count on her own memories, she would hardly be the same person. Moreover, the board here would be able to manipulate an imperial agent. She would have rather died than been in these men's grasps.

As Zarmol readied the dispenser in his hand, the door opened one more time. He looked up, distracted by the *whooshing* sound of the automatic opener. "We have a private matter here. You'll have to come back later to use the— Wait a moment, who are you?"

He received the answer in the form of a laser blast to his face. Zarmol collapsed to the ground, smoldering, the scent of burning flesh filling the room.

Ayla had smelled the awful odor enough times in her day where she had become desensitized to it, though she still tensed in surprise to find someone shooting Zarmol down. The spore dispenser fell harmlessly to the floor, *clacking* on the surface but not activating its contents.

A shadow fell over her, and then a person's face filled her vision, upside down from her view.

It was Mihael. He stood over her with a wry grin. "What kind of mess did you get yourself into?"

Ayla breathed a sigh of relief. She had thought all hope was lost, a terrible feeling, and one she had experienced before, but she had backup. "I don't know. I went to bed and some men grabbed me and brought me here. I don't suppose you can remove my restraints?"

"I should charge you a share of the profits," Mihael said, moving to the controls, and then unlocking her clamps a moment later.

Ayla sat up, rubbing her wrists and squeezing her fist shut. Her arms had fallen asleep from the way she'd been positioned. "We should get out of here before someone comes looking for Zarmol," she said.

"I'm in agreement with you. It took some doing sneaking into here, but I know the way back out. We'll have to do our best not to draw any attention," Mihael said.

"I'll try," Ayla said, sliding off the table and onto her feet. She had trouble with not attracting attention, merely because of the way she looked. It was a blessing and a curse.

Mihael led her out of the room and into the hallway. Fortunately, Dorrinal didn't cross their paths as they pushed through the different areas of the compound.

They made their way past the large machinery room, other lab workers taking no notice of them as they passed. Mihael had holstered his blaster pistol as to not be suspicious. It looked like they would have smooth sailing out of this place.

Finally, they reached an exit to the building, which revealed a large courtyard, parking for flitters, a decorative fountain, and a fence keeping the area enclosed. They were outside but not free yet.

Security spotted them a moment later.

"Freeze!" a man shouted.

"That's our cue to run," Mihael said. He took off bolting as quickly as he could toward a guard station at the front of the fence.

The security guard at the station exited his booth, pointing his blaster pistol at them. Ayla ran after Mihael, right toward the lone guard, and away from the voice yelling for them to stop. She snuck a glance behind her, spotting two more security guards. It wouldn't be easy to escape here and, once they did, they would probably have to deal with all too many local officials.

At least the only person who seemed aware of who she was and why she'd been there was Zarmol. He couldn't tell anyone about her.

Blaster fire erupted around them, but the shots blew by her as she ran, and others fizzled at her feet. They approached the guard station fast enough that Ayla was able to slam the weapon out of the security guard's hand before he could fire at them. She shoved him back into his booth, which caused him to lose his footing.

It gave them a clear path of escape into the city. Mihael kept running, and Ayla maintained pace with him. The guards behind them pursued, firing their blasters a few more times, but Mihael eventually came to another building and rounded the corner, giving them cover from the fire.

People in the streets took notice of them, shouting, pointing, making a scene, but Mihael and Ayla paid them no mind. They kept going until Mihael motioned toward an alleyway, and they disappeared down into it.

The shadow of a building concealed them, and they hid behind some boxes. Mihael pressed a finger to his lips to instruct her to be quiet, and they both looked around the boxes to get a view of the streets.

Security guards jogged by on foot, not seeing them in the alleyway. They were safe for now.

Ayla leaned against the building and let out a sigh of relief. She glanced at Mihael.

"We're not heading back to their little residence, are we?" Ayla asked.

Mihael laughed. "Of course not. They'll probably have a team waiting for us to bring you right back to the lab. We'll return to the ship and lock ourselves in. Hopefully, this will blow over. I hope you didn't cause them too much damage."

She wanted to reply back with, "You're the one who killed Zarmol," but she wasn't about to be too flippant with the man who rescued her. Instead, she followed his lead and waited until it was safe to come out and head back to his ship.

16

Ayla stepped onto the deck after Captain Mihael. It had been a few days since she'd flown on the *Peregrine*. Even though she hadn't spent a lot of time there, it felt considerably safer and like home than anywhere she'd been on Zenda. The Robeni pirates, as much as they were criminals, had a code of honor to them. They looked out for each other.

Jannik greeted them in the cargo bay, dutifully at his post as he stood behind a console that raised and lowered the ramp to the outside. It was a simple job and probably didn't require someone to be there, but Mihael liked to have someone standing guard for the ship. It never hurt to be safe from trespassers.

Mihael grunted in response to Jannik, passing through and heading into the corridor. He didn't turn or say anything to Ayla, but she had the feeling she was supposed to follow him, and so she did, making her way into the small spaces of the ship, and then turning into the kitchen area and the lounge.

Tanya loaded the dishes into the washer, looking up at Ayla as she entered with Mihael.

"Back on the ship? Did we get the goods?" Tanya asked.

"Nothing yet," Mihael said, not sounding too happy. "We've had a little trouble in keeping our crew intact. I don't trust the people here."

"Well, we *are* on a world listed with no population nor development, and yet there's a whole civilization here," Tanya said.

Mihael moved around the counter, getting himself a glass of water and taking a long gulp before setting it down again. Then, he looked up toward the chef. "Tanya, if you would give us a moment?"

Tanya narrowed her eyes at him but nodded. "Of course, captain," she said, lingering on the last word. She brushed passed him and made her way out the door, leaving Mihael and Ayla alone.

Ayla crossed her arms across her chest, not sure why Mihael wanted privacy. He'd rescued her on his own, was he expecting some kind of compensation? Perhaps in the form of physicality? She searched his eyes, but when he looked at her, he didn't seem to be gazing at her with any kind of lovelorn interest.

Mihael stepped from behind the counter, and he had his blaster pistol in his hand, pointing it toward her, lips shut pencil thin. No, he was looking at her as if she were hostile.

All Ayla could think to do was to put her hands up. "Don't shoot?" she asked wryly. "I'm unarmed."

"Not less dangerous, if I'm right about my hunch," Mihael said. He kept his laser pistol steady. "I'd thought the story of a renegade duchess was too suspicious this entire time, and your personality doesn't play with the type of a royal. You don't act spoiled, you don't act flighty or like we're your peons. No, you carry yourself like someone trained, professional. A duchess from an agrarian planet would never act like you."

"You've met many nobles?"

"I've seen enough."

Silence fell between them. This wasn't good. The pirates could be nearly as dangerous as Zarmol had been when she'd blown her cover by sending an ansible message to her handler. But she hadn't blown cover in this situation. This was Mihael having a suspicion about her. A valid one, as she hadn't played the role of a spoiled aristocrat well enough. She even could see that in hindsight.

Ayla had wanted to ingratiate herself to the pirates, to help them with their mission and, by proxy, hers. By doing so, she'd not kept character well enough. She would have cursed to herself, but that only would have further implicated her.

"You seem to have all sorts of ideas floating in your head, but I'm me. People have been suspicious of me all my life. Even Zarmol didn't like my snooping around, which, I might add, was done for you and your ship," Ayla said. "I'm not sure what you're trying to say."

"I'm trying to say you're not being honest with me. You're playing word games. I'm not the most educated man out there, but I have a street sense like none other. Olderman might be fooled by a pretty face, but I'm not. I've watched you. You're scanning the room at all times, listening on conversations more than ten meters away. You watch the exits. How you've acted when you saw the immortality spore being applied, well, let's just say it was far more than an interest of someone who's trying to score a quick payday and resolve her daddy issues." Mihael paused. "But you should know, this is not a court of law. This is my ship. I am the law here. If I smell something foul, I'll boot you right out, or I might even disintegrate you here with old faithful." He waved the blaster pistol in front of her to solidify his point. "Now, I'm giving you one more chance to tell me the truth—the real truth—or you're going to be in for a world of hurt."

Based on their positions, Ayla estimated that she could likely duck out of the way of any fire and still be able to incapacitate Mihael. He had a good bead on her, but any scuffle likely would have resulted in her winning. At least, when it was just them. Then, with the commotion, she'd have to fight past the other pirates.

And then what? Escape to Zenda? This was a hostile world where she'd already gotten into far too much trouble. With Zarmol dead, the men in the lab would probably have her on some kind of security cameras to where they would have her image. It would be a manhunt with no way to escape this place. She couldn't afford to lose the protection of the pirates.

It was the flaw in the mission, one which may well prove fatal. Jorus had rushed her out into the fringes of society, and she'd gone along with everything that had come along the way. Each stop along her journey she'd thought it'd been too easy, and it had been. Now, she stood at a crossroads, unsure what to do.

Could she trust Mihael? The pirates had a sense of honor of sorts, so she had thought before. Even with his suspicions, he had also taken the risk to rescue her from the lab, where she'd been kidnapped under the clutches of the board controlling this planet. She was already in about the most precarious situation she could imagine.

She didn't know the pirate captain well enough, however, to gauge how he would react to finding out she was truly an imperial agent. Pirates didn't generally like the government very much. Her people tended to be bad for their businesses. But there was too much at stake here.

With the spore not only threatening to disrupt the stability of the Imperium with its anti-aging effects, and now it having even further repercussions by tampering with people's memories, it was too dangerous to allow herself to fail. Not to mention the mysterious person in the environment suit who was clearly trying to start some kind of treasonous rebellion. She had to put a stop to it.

And she wouldn't be able to do it without help. She at least had to stall for enough time for the space Marines to arrive, if Jorus had indeed dispatched them, something else she couldn't be certain would come to fruition. Even though every fiber of her being screamed she should be fighting and fleeing from Mihael, her rational sense told her she had no choice but to trust him. She would tell him the truth.

"Well?" Mihael pressed her.

Ayla let out a deep breath, locking her eyes with his.

"I'm an agent for the Terra Prime Intelligence Agency. I was sent to investigate because we received reports of the pirates coming to exploit an eternal life miracle drug. Turns out the reports were true, and it led me here with you. I don't know anything about this planet or anyone here anymore than you do. When Zarmol kidnapped me, it caught me off guard because I wasn't expecting a direct threat."

Mihael burst out laughing. "Good one."

"I'm serious!" Ayla protested.

"You're serious?" He sounded as if he wasn't too sure about her sincerity. The pirate captain narrowed his eyes at her, and then looked to his gun.

"I've been genetically modified for reflexes and reaction times. The second you move to fire, I'll notice, and I'll have the gun pried from your hands and you incapacitated," Ayla said.

Mihael lowered his gun. "Let's say for the sake of argument I believe you. Why should I let you out of here? You might be able to take me down, but I doubt you could handle the entire crew. Not to mention this entire planet might be up in arms over you by this time."

"Because you know very well this spore is dangerous, and if it gets out and into the wrong hands, we're going to be dealing with a populace with no capability for rational thinking and that can live forever. It's going to upend our entire society."

"You really believe that?"

"You don't?"

The silence between them was interrupted by the sound of boots falling upon metal in the corridor outside. It passed a moment later.

Mihael furrowed his brow and frowned. "I agree with you. It's been unsettling since we landed, and now we've seen too much for me to want to be a party to this, even if there are profits to be had."

Ayla offered a small smile at him. "I knew you were a man of honor at heart. A pirate with a moral code. I lucked out on my ship placement."

"That you did." Mihael moved over to the kitchen counter, reaching around to grab a bottle. He popped the top of it and took a swig directly out from it, not bothering with a cup. He may have had some honor, but he still was a somewhat uncivilized man. "The crew isn't going to like this."

"They'll follow your orders. They trust you. And I'm sure if we explain how dangerous this spore is to people, they won't want a part of it either."

"I think you underestimate people's profit motive," Mihael said.

Ayla held out her hand expectantly, wiggling her fingers toward the bottle.

Mihael handed the bottle over.

"From my brief interactions," Ayla said, taking a sip, "your crew are good people. I'd almost say you hand-picked them because of such, but then you got assigned me."

"My luck," Mihael said. "What do you propose we do next?"

Ayla took a small swig of the liquid. It had a sweetness to it followed by some heavy alcoholic aftertaste. This wasn't the fine wine she was used to partaking in back on Terra Prime. But she could handle it, nonetheless. She handed the bottle back to the pirate captain.

"There was a man in an environment suit who seemed like some kind of mastermind wanting to use this to enslave a population to his bidding," Ayla said.

Mihael chuckled. "That sounds like a villain from a holo."

She shrugged. "Maybe so, but it's what we're dealing with. I'm sure such a suit would stand out. If we can do some recon and find him, that would be the first step to ensuring this is taken care of. Other than that, I called for backup. We just have to wait until the space Marines arrive and take care of business."

"I don't want to be here when that happens. Those overblown space cops don't appreciate Robeni pirates."

"I'll make sure no one hassles you," Ayla said. "You're deputy agents of the Imperium now."

"Just what I always wanted," Mihael snapped and took another long swig.

17

Rams pulled Dorrinal by the shirt and yanked him into the alley. The pirate's biceps flexed, skin showing through his sleeveless shirt as he pushed the scientist against the wall behind him. Ayla stood with Jannik, who Mihael had sent on this mission to "gain experience," as per his words. As much as she didn't like newbies to be engaging in more dangerous elements of missions like kidnappings and assaults, she felt obliged to honor Mihael's requests.

So far, Jannik hadn't added to the mission, all he did was stand there behind Ayla, as if she were the one to guard him.

Rams, by contrast, had a rather hands-on approach. He cocked his free arm back, balling his fist, threatening to sock Dorrinal in the face.

Dorrinal did his best to raise his arms to block any blow, squirming with panic. "Please, don't hurt me. I'll give you credits. Whatever you want!"

Ayla stepped forward, taking a position toward Rams' side. "My colleague doesn't want to hurt you, and we don't want your credits. We're just looking for a little information. Do you think you can help us?"

The scientist stood wide-eyed, confused. He looked like he didn't recognize her. "Help you with what?"

Someone had tampered with Dorrinal's memory chip again. Sadness welled inside of Ayla. This man hadn't done anything wrong, only tried to work and do what he'd been told. As a price for his loyalty, he'd been stripped of what he'd known. How many others on this planet suffered the same fate?

"Release him," Ayla said finally, but then pointed to Dorrinal. "Don't you dare try to run."

Rams dropped his grip on Dorrinal's shirt. The scientist rubbed his chest, and then held his hands up. "Listen, I don't know what's going on. I just work for the spore factory as a scientist. I'm helping the people of this planet evade death."

"And we want to help, too. There's some bad actors out there trying to get this spore and...uh, use it for nefarious purposes." She glanced at Rams.

He shrugged in return.

"How could it be used for nefarious purposes? It heals people."

"I know you don't know me, but you have to trust me." Ayla's eyes fell back on him. She tried to win him over with a small smile. At one point, he had found her attractive. Surely, the spore couldn't erase basic human instincts along with the memories.

His expression seemed to soften toward her. "Okay. I don't know why you had this guy grab me, though."

"We're in a hurry. Couldn't risk missing you." Ayla placed her hands on her hips. "Now, listen to me. Zarmol, the council member, was meeting with a fellow in an environmental suit before. That's the nefarious fellow. He's duping your board here. I need to find out who Zarmol's replacement is on the board so we can find him and make sure this environmental-suited fellow doesn't harm him."

Dorrinal narrowed his eyes, clearly not exactly trusting of her, but he sucked his bottom lip in. "I think you're talking about Tylon. He was the deputy operations officer in charge, and the board promoted him, at least temporarily."

Ayla turned to look at Jannik.

The young pirate tapped into his datapad and pulled up a picture. It was a younger man, curly brown hair, skinny, with brown eyes. He had a chip under his right cheek. Jannik held the datapad up to Dorrinal. "This him?"

Dorrinal nodded.

"All right," Jannik said, tapping into the datapad once more. "I think I've got his apartment location."

"Thank you for your help," Ayla said, spinning on her heels. She motioned for Jannik and Rams. "Lead the way."

"That's it?" Dorrinal asked.

Ayla turned, her hair flipping over her shoulder. She gave him a warm smile. "Until next time. Thank you, Dorrinal."

"But how did you know my name?"

The question lingered as Ayla and her friends walked away, following Jannik's lead toward the residential section of the city.

18

ONCE THEY HAD SCOUTED THE RESIDENTIAL AREA WHERE TYLON LIVED, Ayla decided it would be best for them to get a vehicle, look inconspicuous, and watch from across the street to be able to tail him and see if she could run into this environmental-suited individual.

They rode in a small transport car for hours. Jannik sat in the back while Ayla and Rams stayed up front. Ayla's glasses provided a binoculars-style view where she could zoom in on the door and get a good look to see who entered and exited the building.

For the hours they'd been sitting there, Tylon hadn't come out of the building, but he had to have been home based on his work schedule.

Her stomach started to grumble, but she didn't want to leave. They'd been there so long already, and Tylon had to arrive at his home at some point.

"We should have brought snacks," Ayla said to herself.

Rams snorted.

Ayla turned to him, grinning. "You're a snorter when you laugh? I wouldn't have imagined."

The bigger man narrowed his eyes at her. "You tell anyone, I'll snap your neck."

"No, you won't," Ayla teased.

Jannik laughed, too. "You sound ridiculous."

Rams made a move like he was going to punch Jannik, and the younger pirate ducked into the back seat, almost in a fetal position.

The absurdity of the situation made Ayla laugh, and Rams followed with another snort.

"I can't believe it. Jannik's right. You look and sound ridiculous. And I know you won't hit me, so don't even try it," Ayla said.

Rams grumbled to himself, turning to face forward. "Don't tell anyone."

"Secret's safe with me," Ayla said.

A few more minutes passed, and someone appeared at the door, opened it, and stepped outside. The man matched the picture of Tylon she'd seen earlier.

"Hey, Jannik," Ayla said, motioning her head toward the entryway of the building. She didn't want to point, as making overt gestures tended to draw too much attention. "This him?"

Jannik fumbled for his datapad in the back of the transport and held it up. "Yes, most definitely!"

Ayla watched as Tylon went about his day, strolling down the street with no sense of being watched. She activated the transport's drive, lifting them up about ten stories above where they had been prior. It was much easier to follow someone from a bird's eye view position, the vertical axis giving them both a good perspective to make sure they didn't lose their target and ensuring the mark didn't spot them.

She drove along at a distance behind Tylon while he wove his way through the streets, heading in a different direction than he would have if he were to have gone into the spore processing facility.

The way seemed familiar, even though Ayla looked at it from a different perspective from when she had walked the streets. Where was this man headed?

He stopped on a street where Ayla recognized. She couldn't recall it at first until she spotted the Shamrock Pub, the ancient Earththemed bar she'd visited when the pirates and she first arrived on Zenda.

Tylon made his way inside.

Ayla lowered the transport to ground level and parked about a block away. She couldn't see inside, but she knew where the target had gone. If she was on her own, she would have staked out the place herself, but she felt obliged to call Mihael and give him an update. She booted up the car's comm system.

"Hello?" Mihael answered from the other end.

"Captain, we've reached our target, a new member of the board named Tylon," Ayla said. "We're following him on a hunch that he might be meeting with our mysterious enviro-suit man. Eventually, I figure he'll make contact, and we'll be able to uncover who's behind this operation."

"I can't believe I'm letting you use my people for this."

"We'll make sure you get compensated," Ayla said.

"Right."

Mihael hadn't told the others about her allegiance to the emperor, keeping her secret in confidence. Her hunch about his sense of honor was correct so far.

"Don't worry," Ayla said, "I just have to figure out how to tail him. He's gone into the Shamrock Pub. I'd go in, but I don't want to be recognized."

"Hang tight, I have just the plan," Mihael said. "I'll meet you in ten."

"Got it," Ayla said before the comm went dead. She wasn't sure what Mihael had in mind, but she figured she'd trusted the pirate this far. He seemed to have a good head on his shoulders, when he wasn't drinking too much.

Mihael arrived when he said he would, with a big duffle bag slung around his shoulders. He tapped on the transport window, jolting Jannik into sitting up straight in the back seat.

Ayla lowered the window. "Fancy meeting you here," she said.

"You're not very inconspicuous," Mihael said, glancing around. "I'm surprised there's not some planet-wide search out for you given the mess you got us into earlier."

Ayla shrugged. "The person who would have led it can't exactly call for one at this point."

"You're welcome. Hop out of the transport. We'll go in together," Mihael said. He inclined his head toward Rams and Jannik. "You two stay here and be ready in case we need a quick getaway."

"Got it," Rams said.

While they talked, Ayla opened the door and slid out of the driver's seat. She stood in front of Mihael. "We're going to walk in here like this?"

"No, I brought disguises." He ruffled through the duffle bag and produced a long cloak, handing it to Ayla. A second one appeared in his hands moments later, and he chucked the bag into the transport before putting the cloak on and pulling up a hood.

Ayla gave him a skeptical glance. "You think putting hoods over our heads is going to ensure we don't draw attention? If anything, I'd say it makes us look suspicious."

"Suspicious, maybe, but will they be looking for suspicious? Or will they be looking for your red hair?" Mihael tugged on the cloak and smoothed it down. "It makes us look dangerous and like we're people not to be trifled with."

"If you say so," Ayla said, putting her arms through the holes while Mihael held it out for her, and then shrugging the cloak onto her shoulders. She pulled the hood up.

Mihael stepped back to survey her. "Perfect. I wouldn't recognize you at all."

"You have to be kidding me," Ayla said.

"Not in the least. Come on. We don't want to miss the mark." Mihael walked with a pirate's swagger toward the bar.

Ayla glanced back at the transport and the pirates inside. Jannik gave her a friendly wave before she jogged to catch up to Mihael. "I can't help but think this is a bad idea. There's no way we're going to go unnoticed."

"Trust me, I've done this kind of thing before," Mihael said.

"So have I!" Ayla protested, stopping at the bar's entrance. "And, usually, I go in with a better plan. A changeling mask to obscure features. A genetic mod to change my hair color. This is amateur hour."

"When you're out on the fringes with nothing more than your crew, you make do with what you can," Mihael said. He opened the door and held it for her.

His maneuver ended the discussion between them, as Ayla wouldn't continue an argument when there were people around. That would draw far too much attention. Still, she couldn't help but think this was about to lead to a precarious situation.

19

Mihael couldn't help but tug on his cloak as they entered the bar. It would draw attention to them.

Ayla muttered to herself about getting caught, but this time, the Shamrock Pub had a much larger number of patrons than it had when they first had gone to the bar. The same waitress served drinks, but she didn't take notice of them. The packed house of patrons kept her busy.

The floor had a sticky texture. Someone had spilled something earlier, and Ayla lifted her boots carefully, each step making a *creak* sound as she couldn't help avoid it. Another small nuisance to draw attention to them.

Tylon sat at a table alone. Another table was empty beside him, allowing for the perfect place to eavesdrop.

Ayla and Mihael picked up their paces, sliding into the seats before other customers could get a chance to notice the table and try to steal it for themselves. Ayla scanned the room again, noting it was the last free table. They'd been lucky, so far.

A different server arrived at their table than the bartender Ayla had recognized. Even though the woman wouldn't remember them without activating her chip, it gave Ayla some comfort to know they weren't going to get spotted so easily. These disguises were amateur at best, and it made her uncomfortable to sit there.

Mihael ordered two whiskies for them, which made Ayla raise a brow as the server departed.

"An aggressive drink order for this time of day," Ayla said.

"It's drinking time somewhere," Mihael replied.

Tylon received a lighter drink option, with a frothy beer stein arriving at his table as they discussed Mihael's order choice. The pirate could hold his liquor more than most, but he also became a liability when he drank, which Ayla wanted to avoid if possible.

Their mark worked on his datapad, oblivious to his surroundings for a long while. Everything had worked well so far, but they would have to see how this situation went as the day progressed.

Patrons came and went, glasses filled and emptied, but the bar maintained a steady flow of activity. They must have come on an off night the first time, Ayla surmised.

"You know what?" Mihael asked, breaking Ayla's train of thought on the mission. The pirate had already finished his whiskey in the time they waited, and he ordered another.

"Hmm?" Ayla asked, turning her glass to the side. She'd barely sipped her first drink, not much of a hard alcohol drinker, especially when she wanted to have her wits about her for a mission.

"I fashion myself something of a loyalist. I know that sounds ridiculous given my profession," Mihael said.

Ayla couldn't help but chuckle. "You know you subvert the laws of the Imperium for a living. If situations were different, I might be hauling you in for extradition to a prison planet."

He waved off the suggestion. "I knew you wouldn't believe me."

His eyes had sincerity to them, twinkling at her. Of course, he found her attractive, but he hadn't made any untoward moves, which she appreciated. In many ways, he'd been more gentlemanly than Jorus.

"I believe you," Ayla said, bringing her whiskey glass to her lips reflexively, needing the motion to dull the awkwardness of the situation. She took a small sip. "It's surprising to hear, is all. I had wondered why you were so quick to accept my true identity. If you're a loyalist, it makes smore sense."

"Does it?" Mihael cocked his head.

Before she could answer, the conversational sound in the room dropped by several decibels, alerting Ayla to something being amiss. The door opened, revealing the environmental-suited man who she'd seen in the factory. She looked back over her shoulder and noticed several other of the bar patrons ogling the odd sight. The suit drew far more attention than their cloaked entrance.

Whoever wore the suit, he didn't seem to mind the attention. He made his way toward the table with Tylon, who in turn stood to greet him. The suited man towered over Tylon, looming at almost seven feet. As tall as the suited man was, he appeared to be thin even with the armor. The suit had a breather attached with an exhaust tube, which Ayla hadn't had time to get a good look at the first time she'd seen the suit.

"Glad to see you. I'm not sure why you requested to meet here instead of the facility," Tylon said, motioning to the seat across from him as he returned to his own chair. "

"After the most recent incident, I thought somewhere public would be better," the suited man said, his voice modulated as before.

What was he hiding? Why did he go around in such a suit and voice changer? Ayla could think of several reasons. Perhaps he had lung trauma and needed a suit to assist, but it seemed more like a matter of concealing identity than it did for breathing.

"We had a break in. Our investigators are on the matter," Tylon said. "With our world being so remote, Zarmol had some lax security measures, but I assure you it'll change under my watch. We've already identified the trespassing woman and made sure every police agency on the planet is aware of her profile. They'll find her."

The waitress who'd served them on their last visit made her way to their table. She must have been in management to deal with the more important guests. "Can I get you anything?" she said with a small, nervous smile.

"I do not partake in libations," the suited man said.

"I'm good with my beer, thank you." Tylon returned the smile, equally as nervous.

"Pardon for interrupting." The waitress backed away.

Ayla turned her attention back to her glass, ducking her head so as not to catch the waitress's gaze. The last thing she wanted was to have someone drawing attention to her. This was good reconnaissance, and Mihael's plan had worked well despite her misgivings about it. She wanted to hear what the suited man had to say, and perhaps identify him. He had plans to subvert the Imperium, after all, and she couldn't allow them to come to fruition.

"You'll need to make sure your facility and your entire planet is in order by the time we are done," the suited man continued once the waitress was out of earshot. "Between this and the talk of resistance against our spore project, my people are getting nervous in your ability to follow through."

Tylon sat up a little straighter. "I can follow through. I'm much more diligent than Zarmol, I promise."

"You've still made no progress in finding this Hervey character?"

Tylon swallowed. "Nothing so far. We're working on it."

Ayla did all she could to resist rolling her eyes. Another inept bureaucracy. She pretended to laugh at something Mihael said to keep up the illusion of their having a conversation, tapping him on the arm.

"Enjoyed that, did you?" Mihael said, not missing a beat.

"Of course, of course. Now, where were we?" Ayla asked, sounding flighty and distant.

The men at the other table appeared to take no special note of them, nor their conversation.

"Let's hope for your sake you are correct," the suited man said. "We are behind schedule, and the entirety of this planet needs to be on the spore by the end of the month. Can you deliver?"

Tylon let out a breath through his nose. "I'm going to try, but I don't want to promise what I can't guarantee. We'll be almost at full compliance. Unfortunately, our tests of a mass aerial distribution failed. The spore needs to be concentrated and fresh from the dispenser to work, so it only can be applied in single-user doses.

Regardless, the few stragglers won't matter. Our next phase will make it impossible to do commerce in any significant way without having a spore-pass. The resistance will find it difficult to keep at it when they can't have access to stores, transportation, or the basic necessities of life. This isn't exactly a planet where you can just forage for food on your own."

"It is a sound plan. Now, were you going to meet again with those pirates who promised to export the spore to the rest of the Imperium?"

"I haven't contacted them yet. Their captain, Mihael, seemed eager to do business before. I'm sure we can provide him incentives to up the timetable. My only concern is our facilities haven't reached the point where we can guarantee enough of exports off world. Didn't you say you wanted this implemented en masse to ensure full adaptation?"

"I did," the suited man said. "You'll let us worry about the next steps. Once one planet is fully immersed, we will do another, then another, and soon, they will all fall."

"Like dominoes," Tylon said.

"I do not understand."

"It's an old Earth game, invented before the move to Terra Prime. The pieces stand on their sides… it's difficult to explain. Forget I said anything." Tylon waved to dismiss the line of conversation. "But I'll do what I can to keep the pirates on board. If they need some pocket greasing, that should be easy enough. And then we'll make sure they transport the spore to the target world of your choice, everyone's happy."

"Excellent," the suited man said. "You are enthusiastic and a good worker thus far. If you keep this up and deliver on what you say, the Darmarin will reward you. Perhaps you will be the arbiter of this world."

"Well, I'm already on the council," Tylon said.

"Arbiter would be a solitary position."

"Ahh." Tylon raised his glass toward the suited man.

"What are you doing?"

"It's called a toast. You... Never mind. Another cultural item to explain."

Ayla could hardly maintain her own phony conversation at this juncture. Who were these Darmarin? She filed the name away in her head, grateful she had the capability to process memories still. Zarmol hadn't been too far from taking it from her.

She wanted to call Jorus again, update him with this information, but if she made a call off planet from the ship, she would surely be traced at this juncture. Too many people knew who she was—and they would be looking for her, if Tylon had the correct information.

Regardless of who the Darmarin were, this suited man promised Tylon what sounded like his own emperorship. It constituted treason, more than enough for her to shut down this entire planet, if she had space Marine backup. Jorus hadn't given her a guarantee for how long they would take to get here. It could be days, or it could be weeks, but she wanted to shut this down as quickly as she could with so many of the population getting sucked in by the immortality spore.

The spore had no purpose other than to purge people of their memories and create a population under control of the Darmarin. It was clear now. She couldn't let this go on, regardless of when the Marines would make it to the planet.

"That will be all for now. I'll be in contact with my people, ensure you receive the resources you need for the next phase of production, and we will be in touch in another week's time, yes?" The suited man rose from his position at the table.

"Yes. I—" Tylon blinked, zeroing in on Ayla with narrowed eyes. His face lit up with recognition. "I know you. The girl from the factory. She's the wanted woman!" He stood and pointed to Ayla.

Mihael reacted quickly, flipping over the table. He scrambled, spilling another table's drinks on the patrons, pushing them into another table. He then grabbed his glass off the floor and threw it at the bar.

"Bar fight!" he shouted.

The entire place erupted into panic as people shot up from their tables, pushing each other. Arguments broke out. The waitress tried to calm everyone down by yelling, but it only exacerbated the situation.

Mihael grabbed Ayla by the arm, learning in to whisper into her ear with his hot breath. "Start the fight, sneak out. Old pirate's trick. Let's move."

Ayla followed him as he dragged her through a crowd of people. They made it to the door without anyone stopping them. She looked back, and it seemed like the man in the environmental suit stared at her, though she couldn't see his face. It gave her the shivers before Mihael whisked her out into the evening air.

20

Mihael and Ayla rushed back into the pirate ship, followed by Rams and Jannik. It looked like no one had followed them, but with surveillance in cities, one could never be sure. Ayla knew she'd been spotted, and her features had been analyzed too many times. She'd become a liability to the overall mission.

Which was what now? What could she do to save this world before the space Marines arrived? She had to figure out a way to stop the immortality spore from being spread. It was a Trojan horse, a way to destabilize the planet, and then the Imperium.

If she hadn't happened to be on Zenda at the time the spread of the spore came to a peak, the emperor would have never known about this conspiracy and never been able to handle it. There was still a threat of these evil men's plans snowballing throughout the galaxy.

At the very least, millions of lives remained in the balance. Ayla had to save them before it was too late.

The team made their way back into the lounge, where Mihael opened a bottle of whiskey, pouring himself another drink, which he downed. He refilled his cup and turned to the others. "Anyone for a drink?"

"I'll take one," Rams said.

"Me, too," Jannik said.

Mihael looked at Jannik. "Are you old enough?"

"We're pirates. What's that supposed to mean?" Jannik said, standing a little taller to try to look menacing.

Ayla couldn't help but laugh. "I'm glad you can still have a little fun in the middle of a crisis."

Tanya, having been behind the counter as they walked in, brought out several more cups to place them in front of them all.

Mihael poured four more drinks. Each of the pirates took a cup, but Ayla only looked at hers skeptically.

"I didn't tell you I'd be partaking," Ayla said.

"Get over it, princess." Mihael nudged the cup closer to her.

Ayla took it into her hands, not sure if she would drink or not. She didn't want to risk any bad decisions, or sluggishness in the event some of the local authorities came storming into the ship looking for her.

"We're in a tight situation," Mihael said, addressing all of them as if this were some formal speech by a military commander. Though, as someone who'd had a few drinks and started a bar fight, he had a different air to him than any Imperial Space Fleet dignitary.

"I know that much," Rams said. "You ran out of that bar faster than I've ever seen before, and we've been in some tricky situations. What's happening?"

"The immortality spore we've been sent to procure, well, there's problems with it. We've talked about how it messes with people's minds," Mihael said. "It's far worse than that. It strips people of their humanity. I'm all for a little recreational fun and transporting contraband, but this is something completely different."

Tanya took a swig of her drink. "It sounds like you're telling us there's no money to be had."

Mihael looked down into his cup, frowning. "No. It's best we stay away from this whole situation.

"Olderman's gonna be pissed," Tanya said.

The pirate captain turned his attention to the cook, a stern look upon his face. "He's the least of my concerns. All of you are okay with us having a failed mission, abandoning the purse?"

Zahn, the pilot, made his way into the lounge then, yawning and stretching. He hadn't had much to do during their time here, but it would change if they needed to make a quick getaway from the planet. "What's going on? Why the long faces?"

"Captain telling us we're not going to be getting any credits," Rams said.

Zahn stopped in his tracks. "You're joking." He scanned their faces. "You're not joking. What's going on?"

"I was just getting to it. The immortality spore is too dangerous for us to export, and yes, I know it's funny hearing me say this. But it's something bad, and there's even worse forces trying to use this for evil purposes," Mihael said.

"They want to destabilize the Imperium," Ayla said, leaning against the counter. She slyly set her cup to the side, making it look like it was just a natural motion rather than her getting rid of it.

"Isn't that good for business?" Rams asked. "An Imperium with no teeth sounds like freedom for us."

"This one would cost too many lives," Mihael said. "I've seen what this drug does, and how these people get manipulated. I'm not sure who's doing the manipulating, but it's giving me a bad enough feeling I don't want to be involved."

"Some group called the Darmarin," Ayla added.

Zahn's eyes lit up at the word. "Darmarin? I haven't heard of them since I was a kid."

"What do you mean?" Mihael asked.

"I'm from Olpine, it's off any of the major shipping lanes so we have a lot of our own culture. Spacers out there used to talk about Darmarin to kids, like they were boogeymen going to snatch us up in the middle of the night if we acted up. Said they came from the stars, monsters and aliens, part and part. Big and tall, beady eyes." He made a gesture like he was putting fangs in front of his face. "Scared the living daylights out of us like they were bloodsucking vampires or something."

Ayla gulped when she heard the information. This wasn't their first talk of aliens among the pirates. Humanity had never encountered sentient species before. If there was a monstrous alien race out there trying to destabilize the Imperium, this could be something much bigger than she ever considered. It was beyond her pay grade. She wanted to get this intelligence back to headquarters as soon as she possibly could. But there was still the immediate matter of the colonists' safety. Her duty was to protect them as much as anyone else.

"I don't know anything about aliens if they're real or not," Mihael said in between chugs of his whiskey. "I've heard plenty of tales of strange things out on the galaxy's edge, and Zenda is as close to the edge as it gets. Either way, we've got someone throwing that name around to try to scare people, and they don't sound very friendly with what they're planning. I'm not about to be a party to some scheme to overthrow the Imperium, and I think my crew is with me."

Some grumbles and nods echoed his statement around the room, but no one dissented.

"All right," Mihael said. "We're all on board for whatever it is you want to do about this?"

"Why should we listen to her?" Rams asked. "She's just some backwater duchess, isn't she?"

More grumbles echoed in the room but, this time, they didn't sound as positive as when they had been behind their captain's proclamation of mild patriotism.

Mihael looked at her expectantly. "This is your decision."

Ayla was taken aback at how much the pirate captain seemed to respect her. He treated her with courtesy she never would have believed possible from someone in his position. She would try not to betray that kindness he offered her. She cleared her throat. "I apologize for a deception, but I'm not exactly who I said I was when I first arrived here."

Tanya laughed from behind the counter. "Knew it."

"I had a feeling," Rams said.

Jannik shrugged.

Zahn looked horrified. "You're not a princess?"

She'd already told Mihael, and with his crew so loyal to him, Ayla had no nervousness about telling them about her real work. "As I said, I'm sorry. I'm not a princess, nor a duchess. I work for the Terra Prime Intelligence Agency in special operations."

"You were gonna rat us out," Rams said, his body tensing like he was ready to get into a fight.

"Not exactly," Ayla said. "I came here because of the rumors of this immortality spore. Our analysts determined early this would be a threat to the imperium that could destabilize our entire way of life. No one thinks about the long-term implications of a society that doesn't age, doesn't need to retire. It would cause social unrest, but that's the least of the problems. At this point, we know the side-effects of this spore cause people to lose their memory, and that outside forces are using the subsequent implant chips to control what people know. They're doing it in attempt to overthrow the Imperium. We have to stop them."

"We?" Tanya laughed. "I'm here for a paycheck."

Mihael stepped closer to Ayla, protective in his mannerisms. "We all are. And Ayla might be able to arrange us getting paid. Isn't that right?"

"I can see what I can do. At the very least, I know I can grant you some limited immunity for your past transgressions against imperial law."

"What's that supposed to mean?" Rams asked.

"Means she'll clear our criminal records, idiot," Tanya said.

"That would be helpful for getting us past some spaceport securities in different systems," Rams said.

Everyone seemed to agree.

"We want some money, too," Zahn said. "This mission was supposed to be a big payday, and we're getting nothing out of it. I'm just a pilot, but I have a grumbling belly that needs feeding and debts to pay. I can't afford to have spent a week or more for nothing."

"Me either," Jannik said.

Ayla sucked in her bottom lip. She hated promising more than she had the right to, especially given how earnest and forthright these pirates had been with her. It always felt better to deal in subterfuge when handing it out to truly bad people. She found she rather liked these pirates, and so she didn't want to lie to them. "I'll do my best. Until I contact my superiors, I can't promise anything else."

"Good enough for me," Mihael said.

"I'll think about it," Rams said, looking none too happy.

"I'm only in if the money's there," Tanya said.

"Me, too," Zahn said.

Jannik remained tight-lipped, shifting his weight to one foot.

Mihael motioned to the door. "Dismissed."

"This is the lounge," Tanya said, holding her ground.

The pirate captain huffed and stepped forward. "Fine. I'll leave. Ayla, join me." He stumbled forward and headed for the corridor.

Ayla held her head high, trying to maintain a veneer of confidence as she left with the pirate captain. She didn't want to show any signs of cracking. She had to make sure the pirates were willing to follow her, to act like she knew what she was doing, even though it was the handful of them up against an entire planet. The odds weren't good. But they just had to survive until the space Marines arrived while making sure none of the rest of the populace fell to this memory loss scheme.

Mihael fell onto one of the side walls of the corridor, and Ayla had to lock her arm around his to prop him up so he could walk. He'd drank more than he'd realized, having taken shot after shot of the high proof beverage.

"Thank you kindly," Mihael said with a chuckle as their shoulders brushed against one another.

"I've managed drunks before," Ayla said, walking him to his quarters.

It didn't take long to reach his door. The ship wasn't all that big, but the exit from the lounge gave them enough privacy to where it dissolved some of the tension. The others would need time to mull over what they'd heard without her there. It was amazing Mihael had the clarity of mind to suggest it with his state of drunkenness.

When they arrived, Mihael turned toward her. He paused to look at her for a long moment, and then ran his hand through her hair. "Ayla, you are incredible. If someone a month ago would have told me I'd be helping an agent of the Imperium, I'd have laughed them out of the bar. But here we are."

"Here we are," Ayla said.

Upon her reply, he leaned in to try to kiss her. Ayla brought up her hand between them quickly, pressing her index finger against his lips.

"You," Ayla said firmly, "are drunk. Why don't you go sleep it off, and we'll talk again in the morning?"

Mihael made a face of annoyance but turned around, the door opening for him as he stumbled inside.

Ayla leaned against the corridor wall when the door closed. Mihael had fallen for her. It made more sense why he was so eager to help. She was in for another world of trouble.

21

Ayla awoke from a nice sleep in her cabin, finally recovered from her mildly torturous experience with the Zendan lab. The lack of sleep, the fighting and running, the stakeout, it had all caught up to her. But after several hours of peaceful recovery, she was ready to go again. There was a lot to do, but Ayla first went to the 'fresher and cleaned herself up. Some of her pirate friends would do well to do the same, though she wouldn't press them on it.

After making herself presentable, Ayla made her way to the lounge, finding it odd to see it empty for once. The crew spent most of their time there when they weren't in flight, and Tanya had been behind the counter every time Ayla walked in here.

When she went to the bridge, she found it empty as well, but she heard some commotion emanating from the cargo bay.

Ayla sauntered to the bay and found the entire crew glued to a viewscreen toward the back of the bay. On the screen, Tylon stood in front of a podium and a small crowd outside of the facility where Ayla had been held. A line of text blinked at the bottom of the screen with the words, "Emergency Announcement."

This couldn't be good. Ayla stepped beside Mihael, who side-glanced at her.

"Feeling okay today?" Ayla asked.

"A little hungover. Nothing a stim hypo can't handle," Mihael grumbled. He sounded worse than the way he downplayed his state of being. His eyes had dark circles under them. It looked like he hadn't had nearly as restful a night as Ayla.

She wondered if he remembered making a move on her, but her thoughts shifted to current events as Tylon spoke.

"People of Zenda," Tylon said, "thank you for your attention today. We have, over the past few years, seen incredible advancements in our society as more than sixty percent of our world has connected with the natural and healthy spores of this planet to end the horrific disease of aging once and for all. Our people have become the longest living humans ever to walk the galaxy, and we are about to usher in a new golden age of invention, wonder, and positive living."

He paused, and the gathered crowd clapped and cheered for his statement. Ayla had seen propaganda like this before. The group would have been coached on when to applaud in advance to give the appearance of overwhelming support for the government initiatives. One might think such tactics insidious, but optics could be used for good or evil. In this case, it would be the latter.

"However, there's still a large portion of the population who has failed to join us in our quest for bettering humanity," Tylon said, his eyes narrowing, his face becoming much more somber. "Those people, in their selfishness, have been a drain on our society, with medical needs of more than a trillion credits annually. Our system cannot tolerate their self-destructiveness any longer.

"In the past, we have been lenient with people's choices, incentivizing those who would commune with the spore, but our scientists now have done conclusive research of how the spore-deniers would erode our society over time. We cannot allow this to happen. The results would be disastrous. And so, for the good of the people, we are going to be pushing much stricter economic sanctions on those who would not work for the betterment of Zenda. It will be illegal to do commerce without having taken the spore. You will not be able to be employed by any of our wonderful businesses. This is your last chance. You must join us or operate in a self-imposed exile.

"Think of your families. Think of the children. Keep yourselves and them safe, forever. These measures will be enacted within forty-eight hours. You have until then to come to one of our safe spore-dispensaries and inoculate yourselves from the danger of aging. Thank you very much, and may whatever gods you believe in bless Zenda and our future endeavors." He placed his fist to his chest, stepping back from the podium at those words.

The crowd cheered, and several people tried to ask questions, but security took Tylon away, leaving an empty podium and a roaring crowd.

"I can't see this going well," Mihael said under his breath.

"No," Ayla agreed. Something had escalated since the conversation they'd heard with the suited man yesterday. Was the timetable not enough for these Darmarin masters? This amount of pressure to get the people to ingest the spore was borderline insane.

"What now?" Rams asked.

Mihael looked to Ayla.

She carried herself a little straighter. If the pirate captain deferred to her, it essentially gave her command. It was as if she'd commandeered the *Peregrine* on official Imperial business, but different. She was glad the pirates wanted to help her willfully.

"Let me think," Ayla said, sucking in her bottom lip as she considered their next course of action. If the people were going to get forced into taking the spore, there would have to be enforcement, which meant Zenda would deploy some kind of military. She hadn't had enough time or ability to scout the military prowess of the planet. Since Zenda wasn't listed as habited on imperial databases, they did not comply with Imperium regulations regarding planetary militias.

All she could do was worry about what she could control. She had to figure a way to save as much of this non-spored population as she could, keep them safe from these petty tyrants trying to enact their control scheme. But how? She still needed more information.

Ayla let out a deep breath. "Our first course of action should be to get another read on this environmental suit man working for the Darmarin. He's the key to all of this, I'm certain. I wish we'd been able to follow him. It would have been smarter not to just leave the bar like we did."

Mihael grinned. "Oh, it's fine."

"What?"

"During the commotion, I slipped a tracer onto his armor's suit. We have the capability to follow him. It's all tied in with the *Peregrine's* sensors." He inclined his head proudly.

"You are savvier than I gave you credit for," Ayla said.

"I know. It's why I'm the captain," Mihael said.

"Get a room." Tanya snorted and rolled her eyes.

"I've attempted to, trust me," Mihael said, his eyes locking on Ayla with intent.

"*Anyway,*" Ayla said, making sure they didn't drift too far off topic. Every minute could be precious to save lives. "I wish I would have thought of a tracer myself. Well done. Since we have that option, let's try to find where he's at."

"Uh, guys?" Jannik said, standing at his console where he manned the cargo doors and loading mechanisms. He looked down at it as if something were drastically wrong.

"What's going on?" Mihael asked, moving over to the young pirate.

"There's people gathering outside in the spaceport," Jannik said.

"Put it on the main screen," Mihael ordered.

Jannik tapped his controls, and a new image drawn from an exterior camera on the ship appeared on the screen. Over by the fences to the spaceport, a large crowd had amassed. They approached the chain-link fence surrounding the spaceport, keeping people out of the area where ships took off and landed. It was for their own safety. Having people wander onto the tarmac would get them caught in the shockwave of rockets blasting off.

From the looks of the size of the crowd, the fence wouldn't hold forever. More and more people arrived. First hundreds, then thousands. This wouldn't be a safe place to remain for long.

"I think we should get out of here," Ayla said.

"We need to get cleared for takeoff," Zahn said. "If we don't, we've got just as good of odds their air traffic control will shoot us down thinking we're a rogue hostile."

Ayla glanced to Mihael, waiting for him to give the orders.

The pirate captain nodded. "Get the controller on the line. See if we can't get a clearance immediately. Tell them there's a danger to us."

"On it," Zahn said, jogging toward the door and the bridge to get to his comm device.

"We should get to stations and ready ourselves for acceleration," Mihael said.

The others looked none too pleased, but on the viewscreen, the crowd kept growing, and the ones in front pushed at the fence. It swayed under the weight. They didn't have audio, but there had to have been shouting, judging from the looks on the people's faces.

The pirates exited the bay, some going their separate ways, but Mihael, Rams, and Ayla made their way to the bridge following the pilot.

Zahn already sat at his station when he arrived and had the outside rioting up on the viewscreen already.

The crowd pushed at the fence. It tilted. Another wave of them pressed forward, and it finally collapsed under their weight.

Zahn tapped frantically at the controls to get the pre-flight warm up situated.

"Any clearance for departure?" Mihael asked, taking his seat in the captain's chair.

"Nothing yet. Signals are jammed. There's too many ships trying to take off at the same time," Zahn said.

Another ship nearby lifted off, blasting its anti-grav rockets downward into a hard acceleration away. Just as it did, the crowd from outside the spaceport came rushing forward. It was a sea of people, spreading across the tarmac without abandon. The completely sealed walls of the ship isolated them from any sound outside, but Ayla could only imagine how loud the panicked crowd must be.

At first, there didn't appear to be any security around to be able to stop them, but then, in a flash, several small drop ships came down on the tarmac, fully armored Marines popping out of the side hatches of the ship. They didn't conform to the current Terra Prime space Marine armor but had a vestige of something faintly familiar—the distant past. Their standard could've been space Marines from hundreds of years ago. This is what the imperial forces would have looked like back them.

Ayla didn't want to stand around and admire them, however. "I presume your ship has weapons?"

Rams moved over to a station, grunting in response to her.

"Yes. Rams manages those most of the time," Mihael said.

"I might suggest firing a warning shot toward the crowd so they don't get too close to the ship," Ayla said. She knew she was stepping over the bounds of commands, but these were pirates, they might not think as tactically as she would in these situations.

"Do it," Mihael said.

Rams booted up the laser cannons and fired a blast in the direction of the crowd, but several meters in front of them, taking care to not hit anyone. Even though this was a defensive situation, local laws might brand them murderers if they were too aggressive. Ayla didn't say anything to point it out, not wanting to disrupt the flow on the bridge.

"Anything yet?" Mihael asked, his voice filling with more irritation as the crowds came closer. The people outside tangled with Marines, who had brandished blast shields to try to push them back. There weren't enough of the Marines to be able to handle all of them, however. They'd be coming much closer soon enough. The people would be up in their landing struts soon if they didn't move.

"No word," Zahn said, turning back to glance at the captain for further orders. "Pre-launch complete. We're ready to blast off as soon as we have word."

Mihael's face fell into a grimace, understanding full well there were risks and drawbacks to staying or leaving. It was possible the spaceport would try to shoot them out of their air without authorization. It was also possible they would get overrun by the people outside and lose their ship. It wasn't Ayla's call to make, so she allowed the captain his space.

He gripped the sides of his chair, leaning forward. "Mr. Zahn, take off. If they're not going to answer us, we're not going to wait around here to see what's going to happen with this riot."

Zahn swiveled back to face his controls, tapping the console in front of him. "Take off initiated."

The ship rumbled.

22

THE *PEREGRINE* SHOT INTO THE ATMOSPHERE. AYLA HAD TO TAKE A SEAT to make sure she wouldn't fall over and get injured from the force. Even with the gravitational dampeners, the ship was designed to have a smooth ascent, and the additional strain added an excessive amount of weight during the acceleration.

Ayla held her breath. Then, missiles came flying toward them.

"The planetary defense systems activated. Looks like automated heat-seeking projectiles," Rams said, frantically pulling up the missile trajectories onto the main screen for the captain to see.

"Can you shoot them out of the air?" Mihael asked, gripping the sides of his chair tightly.

Ayla had found an unoccupied chair toward the back of the bridge to keep herself secure in during the take off. She had no idea what kind of shielding or armor the pirate vessel had, but she assumed they had to have some defenses. Pirates got entangled in all sorts of combat, didn't they?

"I'm working on it," Rams said. "Can't get a lock right now. We have fifteen seconds before impact."

Ayla couldn't do anything but hold on for dear life. She hated being helpless. If Jorus had only allowed her to take her ship, she could have been in control, knocking out these ancient defenses from Zenda with ease. Imperial technology had quite robust defenses, and her ship was armed to the teeth.

The pirates seemed more than spooked by the prospect of getting hit by missiles. They didn't have anything automated to take care of this. Insanity. Who would fly into space under such conditions?

Desperate people, Ayla thought. She didn't want to have too much empathy for piracy in the Imperium, but after meeting the crew aboard this ship, she started to share some concerns with them and would prefer at least these people survive.

Rams fired the ship's laser cannons. One of the projectiles exploded.

"I've taken out one of the missiles, but the other one is getting too close, I can't get a good sight on its—"

The missile collided with the ship. Nothing rocked, the projectile didn't explode in the air, but it *clanked* against the hull, echoing through the bridge.

Mihael looked up with confusion. "Was it a dud?"

Zahn kept maneuvering, pulling them skyward as much as the ship could bear, but the ship stopped ascending. "Sir, we've got a problem with our engines."

Rams ran scans from his station, narrowing his eyes. "It wasn't an explosive, sir. It looks like the missile clamped onto our hull. It's sending some kind of electromagnetic signal to our hyperdrive, like it's putting a capacitor on it."

"We're not reaching a critical speed to be able to break gravity," Zahn said. "There's nothing I can do."

The missile defenses were meant to disable and bring them in, not to destroy them. Not that the situation made Ayla feel any better. They would have to deal with the government back on the ground, one which was looking for her as a fugitive. They were trapped.

"Incoming transmission from the surface," Zahn said.

"Put it on speaker," Mihael said.

A male voice came through the comm. "Transport ship *Peregrine*, this is Zenda port authority. Return immediately. You have committed an unauthorized launch."

"We didn't have much of a choice," Mihael said. "There was a mob of people breaking down the fence to the spaceport, and they were about to commandeer our ship. We had to leave for our own safety."

"And you'll return until you're authorized to leave. The board has ordered a planet-wide lockdown until we can get the situation under control. Please, set down at landing pad number seven six three. Our representatives will meet you there for questioning. The spaceport break-in has been contained."

Mihael inclined his head to signal Zahn to hit the mute button, and the pilot did.

"Options?"

Zahn shook his head. "Whatever this missile did to our engines, we're not able to get out of it. We're going to be scrambled until we can completely reset our systems, which means a full shutdown groundside. Regardless, we're going to have to touch down."

Ayla grimaced when Mihael looked to her, but she merely shrugged. She didn't know the ins and outs of this ship. All she could do was observe, which she found frustrating, but no more than when the missiles were flying at them, and she couldn't help.

"They're going to inject us with those spores," Rams said.

"Seems about right. How do we avoid it?" Mihael asked.

"The government will attempt to bring us in. Probably with some of their Marines," Ayla said. "We'll have to escape and try to fade into the city somewhere."

"Easier said than done," Mihael said. He turned his attention back to Mihael. "All right, unmute us." He cleared his throat to speak to the operator on the other end. "Okay, we are going to comply and touch down on pad seven six three. Please, make sure no planetary defenses will be coming after us in the meantime."

"You're cleared to land, *Peregrine*. The operator sounded so casual about the matter, like it was another procedural landing. How many other ships tried to leave like they did? A few had departed early into the riots, but had they all been forced to return?

Zahn brought the ship back into landing position, which took several minutes. None of the pirates seemed happy, and Ayla couldn't say she was pleased with this development either.

Mihael looked to Rams. "Did you get a fix on the tracer I put on that fellow in the environmental suit?" He gave Ayla a look. "Might as well keep going with our lead and see if we can find him when we're groundside."

Rams tapped a few controls as Zahn landed the ship. The gruff pirate furrowed his brow. "Interesting. It says he's not on the planet at all but seems to have gone off into one of the system's two asteroid fields. He's on one of the larger ones."

"A base much like the Robeni have," Ayla said.

"Maybe so, but we can't get there now. Zahn, work to reset our system in case we need to try to scramble out of here again. We'll be more prepared next time. I guess we'll meet with whoever they've sent to capture us. Everyone else, follow me."

With the ship landed, Mihael stepped off the bridge. Ayla stood and stuck close behind him, with Rams making his way after.

23

———

When the *Peregrine's* ramp lowered, they were greeted by a dozen planetary Marines in armored suits, led by a woman with a half-shaved head and dark blue hair draping to her neckline on one side. She had the implant chip on her cheek, controlled by the memories the board of this planet would allow her to have. Did any of these people have any understanding they had been made into puppets?

"Exit the transport ship and drop your weapons. You'll be submitting to a search and seizure under the general order of the board," the blue-haired woman said in a low, almost masculine tone.

Ayla had thought about hiding within the ship, trying to extract herself from the situation, but the council likely would have had bioscanners to detect anyone lagging behind. She had to try to blend in and act compliant. With the decision made, she set her laser pistol on the ground, and the other pirates did the same. She had a small hold out pistol in her boot, and she hoped the soldiers wouldn't be thorough enough to search her for it.

They seemed content to leave them with the weapons they had.

"We've been ordered to bring you in for questioning regarding your illegal departure and aggressive actions toward planetary defenses," the woman said.

"The defenses attacked us," Mihael protested, stepping forward. "We were trying to get away from the angry mob attacking this spaceport. Shouldn't you be dealing with them instead of harassing an honest space trader outfit?"

Ayla couldn't help but smirk at the word *honest*. They were certainly the most honest pirates she could have imagined encountering, but she still wouldn't have labeled them as such. Zenda appeared to be going under stricter lockdowns, which made sense given the rioting they'd just encountered. It would be hard to tell friend from foe in those situations, from a governmental perspective. She sympathized but, at the same time, she wished she weren't caught in the middle of this action. Especially as she would have been wanted for her prior encounter with the spore factory.

"Save it for the questioner," the woman said. "Now, is there anyone else aboard the ship?"

"Our pilot," Mihael said.

"Instruct them to come outside."

Mihael slowly took his comm from his pocket as to not spook the Marines into firing upon him, and then he called for the pilot. Zahn joined the party a moment later, not looking too pleased to be out there.

The blue-haired woman motioned for them to proceed away from the transport. The group of Marines parted for them.

Mihael led the way through, keeping his head up. He must have been trying to appear calm for the sake of his crew. Ayla found his demeanor to be admirable in this situation. She certainly found it difficult to keep her cool.

The blue-haired woman turned to walk alongside Mihael, the soldiers flanking the pirate crew on either side as they walked down the tarmac toward a long building with large windows. They approached a ramp and a large door. The soldiers jogged ahead and opened the door for them.

It led to a waiting area inside, which looked like it was for passengers of commercial starliners. There were seats, several holos displaying newscasters giving a report of martial law being declared.

"Residents, return to your home and await this crisis to be over," the newscaster said. "Anyone caught out on the streets will receive fines and possibly jail time. This order has come directly from the board."

The rioting hadn't been isolated to the spaceport if the government took such drastic measures. This meant people rebelled planetwide. The planetary defense forces would be scattered as well, which meant there would be chaos up the ranks, and they would likely be spread thin.

Ayla surveyed the twelve guards around them. The pirates and her might be able to take a few of them out before they were incapacitated, but the problem was, the guards had all the weapons, and they were armored on top of it. Even with her genetic enhancements, she couldn't do much without something else to even the odds.

Could there be something in the spaceport they could use? She glanced around but saw only a large room devoid of people, where the sounds of the newscaster echoed off the hard floors.

"Wait here," the blue-haired woman said. The soldiers with her stopped in their tracks, and the pirates stayed with them.

The woman stepped out of earshot and made some kind of comm call, but she turned so Ayla couldn't read her lips. When the woman returned, she seemed agitated.

"He says he'll be here in fifteen minutes," she said. "Looks like we're going to have to wait."

Mihael stepped toward her, brandishing a sweet smile, something which looked strange on the gruff pirate.

"Listen," the pirate captain said, "this has all been a misunderstanding. As I told you, my people were trying to evade getting our ship overrun by a mob outside who looked like they might hurt anyone they came across who had a spaceship. We didn't mean to violate any edicts or laws. We're not from this planet either. Surely there can be some leniency? We can perhaps make a contribution—"

"Are you trying to bribe me?" The blue-haired woman narrowed her eyes.

Mihael waved frantically to evade the suggestion. "No, of course not. Merely trying to help."

"I don't think it's helping, Cap'n," Zahn said, crossing his arms.

Tanya leaned in toward Ayla, whispering into her ear. "You don't have any plan to get us out of this do you."

Ayla shook her head. They were still outnumbered, more importantly, outgunned. Unless she could separate some of the guards somehow, or find some place of cover they could use, there wouldn't be much point in resisting. The chairs around the area didn't provide an effective shield. All they could do was wait and hope this blue-haired woman's supervisor—or whoever she called—would be more reasonable than she was.

"You should listen to your crew, *Cap'n*," the blue-haired woman said with a distinctly mocking tone applied to Mihael's rank.

Before Mihael could reply, something exploded outside. The blast shattered the windows all around them. Smoke and debris filled the air.

This was the kind of distraction Ayla could work with.

She had to be patient. The opportunity would present itself soon enough, but she couldn't rush any moves or she might make things worse.

The soldiers fanned out, moving in the direction of the blast to take a look outside.

The smoke cleared, revealing a large crowd who moved in this direction. It appeared as if the government hadn't gotten the riots under control despite the proclamation of martial law. They may have pushed them back from the spaceport on the other side, but it merely moved the crowd over toward this area.

Rocks flew in from outside, hitting the soldiers and their armor. They seemed to be okay, but there were far too many people approaching for them to deal with. The blue-haired woman started shouting orders at them, and she took cover behind a nearby empty concession stand.

The room flooded with rioters. Ayla stuck by Mihael, and the soldiers seemed to forget about their captives.

"We can get lost in the crowd if we play this right," Ayla said.

"I'm with you," Mihael agreed. "Everyone, stay close. Let's not get separated!"

The pirates congregated together, fading into the crowd while the rioters pressed forward. If there was an objective for these people, it wasn't clear. They started tearing apart the concession stands and seating, pressing forward into the tarmac area with thousands more behind them bringing up the rear.

With twelve meager soldiers, the government didn't have enough of a presence to stop the rioters. But the problem was, the soldiers had heavy firepower, and they became desperate as the crowd approached them and wrestled for their weapons. One of the laser rifles fired into the ceiling, dropping debris down on the rioters not too far from where the pirates stood.

"We have to fall back into the streets," Ayla said.

"It's like swimming upstream," Mihael said. He took her hand in what seemed a heroic gesture, but it might have been the pirate using the situation to get close to her.

Regardless, she didn't protest. He pulled her along through the crowd, and she went with him. Out the corner of her eye, she saw Tanya and the others not far off to the left.

Then, several shots rang out.

A couple of the soldiers opened fire on the crowd. Unarmed civilians collapsed to the ground. This was going to be a massacre.

Ayla couldn't stop to watch what was going on. She could only hear the cries of pain and the screams of horror as the helpless many were mowed down by the few who had weapons. Eventually, the crowd would be able to overtake them, but Ayla didn't want to be in the line of fire when that happened.

They pushed between people, bumping arms and shoulders, not stopping to give an apology. Even though they nearly trampled over some of the civilians heading the opposite direction, all they could do was keep moving.

The sound of laser fire stopped. The crowd must have overrun the soldiers. Ayla had made it to about the window line on the other side and glanced over her shoulder.

Too many people stood between her and where the soldiers would have been. She couldn't get a good view, but she could imagine what this angry mob would have been doing to them at this juncture.

Served them right, she figured. They should have never opened fire on an unarmed group. This was a travesty. Where was the rest of the planetary police? Their tear gas or stun grenades? Zenda was horribly mismanaged and ill-prepared for a situation like this. They had to have known that trying to force a populace to ingest some strange spores would provoke a negative reaction.

When she made it outside, a shadow fell over her.

It was a troop transport. More armed soldiers dropped from the sides of the vessel. They had jetpacks and hung in the air.

"Clear the area," one said in an amplified voice. "If you do not disperse immediately, you will be subject to arrest or fire. Head away from the spaceport. This is your final warning."

Enough of the crowd heeded the call that it reversed the flow of people. Ayla and Mihael made it out into the streets.

Rams came up beside them as they jogged away. "Barely made it out of there."

"Clear the area. I repeat, return to your homes. Martial law is in effect, and you are in violation of curfew," the amplified voice roared.

Mihael slowed his pace to allow the others to catch up. "I'm not even sure where we can go. We can't get to our ship. We don't really know anywhere around here." He sounded frightened, and Ayla couldn't blame him. They were trapped on a foreign world in a powder keg of a situation. They seemed to have been out of options, though there had to be some abandoned building nearby they could head to and regroup.

She looked around, but there was too much smoke still in the air, and the crowd was scattering every which way. The riot would be breaking up soon.

"I couldn't help but overhear," a man with dark skin and matted black hair said, stepping up toward them. "We want to help everyone without the chip." He pointed to his cheek, which was clear of one of the memory implants. "If you want to follow me, I'll make sure you get to a safe place."

Mihael looked like he was about to protest, but Ayla stepped in front of him before he could speak. She didn't need machismo to ruin a perfectly good situation. This was someone protesting the immortality spore, one of the very people she wanted to help, and she had heard of an organized resistance since coming to the planet. It was time to explore it.

"Thank you so much…?" She trailed off her question, inquiring for a name.

"You can call me Hervey. Come on. Let's hurry out of here before the soldiers take notice of us." He jogged off down the street.

Hervey. The name resonated with her as she'd heard it connected with the resistance group on multiple occasions. Ayla motioned for the pirates to come with her, and she followed.

24

Theʏ arrived in a building which looked to be like any other modern residence, but when they moved past the lobby into a room behind a door, it was anything but a personal home. It looked like a large amphitheater inside a building, hidden and obscured by the decorative lobby and well-placed holonets, which further obscured the visual.

Inside, hundreds of people gathered, all speaking in a low tone. The air felt heavy, angry. Ayla could hardly blame the people for hating the government here. How could a populace deal with trying to be forced into a life without memory? To rely on chips provided by the government to tell them what they were supposed to know.

She could only imagine. If this immortality spore had been exported to the Imperium at large, it could have been a complete disaster for all of humanity. Which is exactly what these Darmarin wanted.

Hervey shook hands with several people around the room, the crowd ready for action. He turned to Ayla.

"I'm going to have to give a speech soon," Hervey said. "We've overwhelmed the planetary forces with protests. They weren't ready for us, but it means they're going to clamp down even harder on what we're doing here. We need to make a statement, fast."

"I have word that the Imperial Space Marines will be on their way. All you have to do is make sure you can keep your people away from the spore, and the Imperium will take care of the rest," Ayla said.

Hervey laughed. "The Imperium? We haven't had anyone from that old crumbling bureaucracy here in hundreds of years."

"Until now," Ayla said.

He raised a brow at her. "You're not just some off world spacer, are you?"

Ayla shrugged. "What gave you that impression?"

"The way you carry yourself."

Mihael nudged her in the side. "You carry yourself like a princess."

"Duchess," Tanya corrected, snark in her tone of voice.

Ayla brandished a small smile. "Well, I'm an agent of the Imperium. This planet became a part of my mission, and it seems there is good reason to be here. Glad I came when I did."

Hervey looked around, exhaling slowly. "I still need something to tell the crowd. We have a win, but we need a good objective."

"How about taking out the spore processing facility?" Ayla asked. She had just been there, and if security forces were spread thinly across the planet, they wouldn't have enough to protect their facility. They probably weren't expecting an attack anyway. It didn't seem like these people had much tactical experience.

"You know, that's not a half bad idea," Hervey said. "I'll get them ready. We have a weapons' cache here we haven't deployed yet—laser rifles, thermal detonators. A few of us were preparing for years just in case the government turned on the people. Looks like we had good reason."

"The Imperium will back you," Ayla said.

She didn't know much about these dissidents, but she knew the current government had more than overstepped their boundaries. The council was a threat to the very people's livelihoods on this planet and, even without vetting Hervey and his resistance group, she had to make the snap decision that they would be better than the alternative. Once the space Marines arrived, they could work a more permanent solution, whether with Hervey in leadership or not, she didn't have to decide now.

Hervey gave a small nod, and then stepped into the center of the amphitheater. The platform in the middle rose, floating in an anti-gravity matrix to allow him to levitate into a raised view with a spotlight on him.

"My friends," Hervey said, his voice amplified by speakers around the room, "we've done well today to let the council know we will not comply with their medical experiments. We're retaining our humanity despite their threats, coercion, and aggression."

The gathered crowd cheered. Ayla politely clapped her hands along with several of the others.

"Our work's not done yet," Hervey said. "Thanks to some offworlders with experience in these matters, they've recommended we complete our resistance by destroying the spore processing facility. I believe with the current state of frenzy of the government and their agents that we can succeed in this. We'll need the people to create a distraction while our militia reserve team places thermal detonators in and around the plant. We'll have these spores go up in smoke."

The crowd roared again. The energy was electric, with people itching for action. The council had stepped too far in declaring martial law, and these people were angry and ready to burn the whole planet to the ground. It was dangerous, but it was also useful for Ayla. So long as she could keep them controlled.

She had little power to do anything now. The suggestion had been made, she could only hope they would stop there and not create a situation where it would lead to endless bloodshed.

Revolutions had been tried before, and they'd failed across the Imperium, but Ayla had never been on the side trying to rise against the government. It felt strange to her, but she was doing so for the greater Imperium.

"Militia team one, meet with me. The rest of you, head out into the streets, draw the security forces away. It's dangerous, I won't lie to you. The government has shown they'll kill their own citizens for their twisted ends. But we will win!"

The crowd shouted their agreements for a third time, louder than ever before. Then, people filed out.

Ayla watched Hervey as he moved to meet with his militia team. She motioned for the pirates to follow her as they weaved through the crowd. As much fun as it sounded to be a part of riots in the streets, she would much rather work on a precision operation to destroy a target. That was her wheelhouse.

She approached the gathered group of militiamen. "Got room for a few more?"

Hervey's eyes twinkled as they met hers. It was convenient how many men would bend over backward for her will, even rebellion leaders. "Of course. Let me tell you the plan."

25

Within minutes, they arrived back on the streets of Zenda. The rioting had taken its toll on the buildings along the streets with window blown out, smoke filling the air, and several fires blazing. Emergency sirens blared, and flitters and drones canvased the skies. On the streets, thousands of people ran amok, some protesting, others causing all kinds of disturbances. It created an electric atmosphere of danger.

Announcements blared through the streets, recorded messages from the council government. "Citizens, return to your homes. Martial law is in effect. If you do not comply, you will be incarcerated or killed."

The message sounded on repeat, grating to hear after more than dozen times.

Cameras had to have been watching the streets, taking note of who was out, who didn't have the memory chip that came along with the immortality spore. The citizens here took a big risk in rebelling, though there seemed to be enough of the population without the chip that the council couldn't make too aggressive moves to control them. If their protest went poorly, they would be caught, and the repercussion to their lives could be immeasurable. If the government went this far to force compliance, they wouldn't be averse to hunting each and every person down.

The militia team made their way through the streets, sticking together, moving at a reasonable speed but deliberately. Local law enforcement didn't seem to single them out beyond anyone else taking to the streets, but there were so many people it would have been difficult for the government to determine who would be a greater threat.

Ayla kept her eyes peeled anyway. Looks could be deceptive, and the council could easily swoop down with all kinds of military machinery that would take mere moments to deploy. One kept alive in situations like this by remaining alert.

Mihael seemed to be equally cognizant, keeping quiet, but scanning the area as they made their way back toward the facility where he'd rescued Ayla from only days before.

They arrived at the guard gate, which had a solitary man standing watch with a laser rifle. He wore a white uniform and, as their entire team approached, his eyes went wide.

"Drop your weapon, and we'll leave you be," Hervey said, flanked by militia members who held their own laser rifles.

The man didn't need further encouraging, taking the sling off his shoulder and placing his rifle carefully on the ground. He stepped backward, and then ran as quickly as he could away from the group.

"You shouldn't let him go," Ayla said, weaving between some of the militiamen to make her way toward Hervey.

"We don't want to harm anyone if we don't have to. Citizens of this planet are all equal," Hervey said. He was idealistic, and as such he risked having this guard alert local authorities. It meant they'd have to get in and out of here that much quicker in order to ensure success.

"If you say so," Ayla said, clutching the laser pistol in her hands a little more tightly than she had before.

Hervey hadn't given Ayla or the pirates any of the detonators. It made sense that they wouldn't trust outsiders with such a responsibility. Instead, they were given arms and instructions to protect the militiamen in their tasks of setting the explosives to blow up the plant.

The team spread out in front of the facility, some setting their devices on the outside walls. They would need to place some inside the large building in the big room with the machinery where Ayla had seen the production of the spore. The resistance couldn't allow the production machinery to survive.

They reached the doors, finding them locked down. A few specialists moved in, planting devices on the doors.

"Step back!" one of them shouted.

The rest of the group moved to a safe distance from the doors.

The devices *fizzed*, and then sparked as they pried the maglocks from the doors and melted down the hinges. Within moments, the noise stopped. The doors fell flat on the ground, crashing hard and leaving the interior of the building exposed.

The facility didn't have the most robust of defenses. The council had no conception that the populace here would fight back. It was the resistance's saving grace, otherwise a frontal assault like this would have had no chance of succeeding.

Several people in lab coats inside fled further into the facility. The scientists didn't want a fight. They were here to do their job, thinking they were providing medical advances for the population here when they actually turned the people into mindless drones. It was insidious, this plan by the Darmarins and the council to force the spores upon the populace. The more Ayla thought about it, the madder she became about the wanton manipulation involved.

The militiamen moved in, along with the pirates. Ayla brought up the rear, glancing toward the gates behind them, expecting that a group of Marines or armored soldiers would appear at any moment, just as they did at the spaceport. So far, they'd been in the clear. Perhaps Hervey's plan of having the larger group distract from their efforts would work after all.

But they also corralled themselves inside the building. Their tight proximity would make them easier to hunt down until they made their way back out again.

"Mihael," Ayla said, motioning the pirate toward her.

He stopped moving. "What are you thinking?"

"Why don't you and a couple of the others stay outside and monitor the situation. If the government arrives, then you can be in a position to make sure we're warned and can get out of here."

"We'll die for the cause if we must," Hervey said, having overheard them.

"You might. I intend to get out of here with my skin intact," Ayla said.

"You heard her," Mihael said to his people. They backed off from the rest of the militia group and made their way back to the entrance.

As they retreated from the main group, security robots appeared in the corridor.

Darts flew from the bots' arms, whistling with the wind they created as they flew toward their targets. Several of the militiamen were hit, the darts piercing their skin. They dropped to the ground. The darts appeared to be sedatives, but Ayla didn't want to take the risk of getting hit and finding out they had some kind of poison in them.

She took cover behind a potted plant at the entrance. These were old-style security bots, humanoid shape to give the appearance of security guards. Three drones flew behind the humanoid bots, surveying the crowd.

The militiamen fell into battle with the bots. Several of them had laser weapons, but the bots had metallic armor that neutralized the shots. They would be difficult to take down.

One of the militiamen jumped onto the bot, knocking it down with his force. Seeing the success, two others did the same. The drones flying overhead fired electric taser bolts at the men on top of the bots, incapacitating them.

"Run for your target locations!" Hervey said. "While they're busy! We might not be able to stop them, but we can slow them down enough to get this done!"

Other men shouted in agreement.

Ayla found it would be good to target the drones. They seemed to be the ones monitoring everything with camera eyes, and without them flying through the air, it would be easier to keep the humanoid bots at bay.

She raised her laser pistol to get a line on one of the cameras. By nature, the glass covering it wouldn't be as well-armored as the rest of the bot. If she could just get herself into a position where she could take aim.

Once the camera entered her line of sight, Ayla pulled the trigger.

The shot connected, blasting the glass out of the drone's lens. It spun around several times before barreling into a wall and falling to the floor. She'd found the weakness. "Target their lenses—on the flying ones!"

The other two drones seemed to sense where the threat had come from, and they flew toward her. They fired their taser lines, but Ayla caught sight of them as the bolts deployed. She rolled across the floor and out of the way. The Taser bolts connected with the plant matter, lighting it on fire when the electricity ran through it.

Smoke filled the air, and soon, the entryway's sprinklers deployed. A foam mist shot out of them, dampening the fire and getting all over everything. In the meantime, one of the militiamen fired upon one of the drones. It connected with the camera lens as well, sending another one spiraling.

The humanoid bots threw off their human weight before flipping back up upon their feet. "You are trespassing on a council-controlled facility. Vacate the premises immediately," a recorded message came from one of the bots.

Several of the other militiamen had already made their way down the corridor. Ayla would have to hold these off here. She hoped that her pirate crew was safe outside. It was better for them to be out of the turmoil anyway. The citizens of this world could handle the bots, with her help at least.

A *crack* resounded.

Ayla scrambled to her feet, turning.

Behind her, one of the militiamen had grabbed a long iron bar and hit the final drone with it. The drone fell to the floor, sparking. The aerial security devices were dispatched. Now, for the much stronger bots.

The humanoid bots grabbed and threw militiamen, they also shot more darts from their arms, incapacitating Hervey's forces by the droves. They'd come in with so many people, but between the splitting up and scattering and now the defense bots doing their work, a paltry few men still stood with Ayla.

Their laser weapons appeared to be useless against these bots. The security drones were designed to face such resistance and shots didn't even slow them down. At least they'd been able to tackle them before and ensure the men who were placing the bombs could get out of this firefight. But they wouldn't be keeping these bots busy for much longer unless they came up with a better strategy.

One of the bots tossed another man against the wall. The man grunted and crumpled to the ground.

Ayla watched, keeping her distance for the time being. There had to be a weakness. Laser fire didn't work, but they could be knocked off their feet.

When the bot turned, she spotted connector patches between its head and its spine. Could it be that easy? If she disabled the lines by the back of its head, would it shut down? There was only one way to find out.

She charged forward toward a bot, slipping and sliding from the fire-retardant foam now on the ground. The bot noticed her, turning to confront her, but Ayla slid under it, between its legs, using its metallic thighs as a hook to stop her momentum and pop back up behind it.

Spinning, Ayla held up her laser pistol. She jabbed the butt of it against the connector of the conduit attached to the bot's cranium. It came loose. She swung again, and the wiring detached.

The bot jolted, and then fell face-forward, crashing to the ground.

"There's two more," Ayla said. "Their weakness is the conduit on the back of their necks. Snap the wires out, and they're done!"

Several of the militiamen still standing acknowledged, engaged with their own bots. The big metallic arms crushed down on one's chest, making him heave as he collapsed, but soon enough the bot was dispatched by one of his compatriots in the same way Ayla had just done. It left one bot remaining.

This time, one of the militiamen tried to distract the bot, waving his arms and flailing, shooting at it. The bot drove forward, focused on his target. This put its back right in front of Ayla. She stepped forward and jabbed the pistol butt at the back of its neck again. This connector was lodged in there.

The bot spun, facing her. It reached out, swiping across, tagging Ayla in the shoulder. The heavy metal hurt when it hit her, knocking her off balance and into a nearby wall. The hit stung, but she couldn't stop now. The other militiaman approached the bot, going for the neck, but the bot sensed it and grabbed him with claw arms.

Ayla had one more opening to get to its neck conduit. She ran forward, jumping and jamming her arm downward onto it at the same time. This time, it unplugged, wires exposed and sparking.

The bot stopped moving.

Before she could even draw a breath, Hervey came back running down the hall.

"The explosives are deployed. Let's get out of here before this place blows!" he shouted.

26

The facility went up in a roaring blast.

Ayla and the others had gotten beyond the radius of the explosion when all of the detonators triggered at once. Even from their distance outside, near to the guard gate, they could feel the reverberations through the air, pushing on them like a gale force wind.

Smoke filled the sky. The rubble of the facility caught fire. Windows shattered in nearby buildings. People screamed, but it all sounded deadened to Ayla, whose ears rang from the intensity of the explosion.

Several seconds passed before she could hear Hervey shouting.

"The Marines are on their way. They know we're here. Scatter!" He took off running without waiting to see who followed.

This was the problem with fostering revolutions. The leadership grew used to being in hiding, and it often ended up a disorganized mess with every man for themselves. If the people organized a little better, and had a little more backbone, they might be able to take on the council's planetary forces.

But they didn't want to risk too much bloodshed.

Ayla caught up to her pirate friends who had been standing guard toward the front of the facility. Mihael waited for her.

"We need to get out of here. Rams spotted dropships landing and creating a perimeter around the facility. They might round us all up to make an example," he said.

Ayla nodded, and then continued past the guard station. She broke into a run along with everyone else around her. She didn't push too hard on her extra-human abilities, wanting to make sure the pirates had a way to keep up with her.

This was an unfamiliar terrain, as much as they had been here for a few days to get the lay of the land. They would be at a severe disadvantage upon a pursuit. But they also had no choice. They couldn't stay here.

Up ahead in the streets, a line of Marines pressed forward. They had blast shields up, and they marched as a unit, not allowing a way for anyone to move past.

Ayla and the others wouldn't be able to go that direction. She halted in her tracks, the pirates stopping along with her. Some of the protestors clashed with the Marines and security forces. They wouldn't fare well without equipment and weaponry. They had some supplies but not on the level of the planetary government.

"We have to find another way," Ayla said.

"Follow me," Zahn said. "Navigating is what I do." The pilot cut between two people and turned the opposite direction down the street. A group of Marines marched there, too, but they had already engaged with several of the dissidents. Their ranks broke, and their line crumbled.

The planetary Marines seemed to be winning the fight against the resistance. Even with the enemy having a personnel advantage, Zahn carved a path between the various battles in the crowd to where they could sneak through, one by one, in a line, trying to get out of the major conflict.

Government operators erected barricades farther down the street. They would be trapped here along with several of the other rebels. The council wasn't messing around here. They had every intention of making example of the people here. It probably upset a lot of the higher ups having their spore-producing facility destroyed so easily.

But that was the benefit of being on a backwater planet. Nothing was well-fortified. The council didn't expect to encounter any real trouble. They'd never quelled full insurrections. Ayla had dealt with such matters personally. There was never a dull day in the Terran Imperium.

There was enough conflict going on, lasers being fired, smoke in the air, where it made it impossible for the government forces to track down any individuals for the time being. So long as they stayed out of the general combat, it looked like they would be in the clear, at least until they were forced into one of the barricades and rounded up.

It was a problem for later. Surviving that long was what mattered now.

A grenade dropped nearby. It exploded with gas, which filled the air around them.

"Tear gas!" Mihael shouted.

It would be too late. They didn't have masks or any filtration equipment. Ayla wished she had her general encounter suit, but being on a covert mission, she didn't have her supplies.

Her eyes watered. They burned. Nothing she could do would stop it despite wiping her face on her arm reflexively. Tears streaked down her face and blurred her vision.

"We have to get out of the main conflict zone," she said.

"I'm trying to find a way," Zahn said. "Zendan forces seem to be everywhere."

Ayla stumbled her way into an alley. There didn't appear to be anyone around there. "Over here," she said.

The pirates migrated over to her, and they all descended into the alley. The street was dimly lit, and also resulted in a dead end. They would have been trapped there but, for the moment, it didn't matter. The tear gas impacted them all too much.

They all cried like they had been at a funeral for one of their best friends, induced by the gas from the grenades. It took a while for the effects of it to wear off, but the pirates leaned against the alleyway walls, staying out of sight of the groups of Zendans of both sides on the streets. It was the reprieve they needed to regroup and figure out what to do.

"Now what?" Tanya asked. "We're stuck here. I don't see a way back to the ship."

"Neither do I," Zahn said.

Mihael frowned. "Maybe we can wait this out."

Ayla shook her head. "They're going to close in on us soon enough. We need an alternative way out of here."

Their brief respite ended as a group of drones descended from the sky into the alleyway. These had some advanced machinery that looked far more sophisticated than what they had encountered with the facility.

One of them shot a net, which spread out and flung toward the pirates. It meant to capture them, force them into a place where they couldn't move. It would keep them incapacitated until they could be arrested.

Ayla dodged the net, as did Jannik, but the others found themselves caught in its web. She took her holdout laser pistol and fired at one of the drone's cameras. The shot connected, her genetically modified reflexes working wonders again, leaving three more drones left.

One flew upward into the air and moved on while the other two remained, like they were guarding their recently captured prey.

"I can't get out of here," Rams said. He flailed within the tangled net, unable to find his way out of it. His resisting only served to bind him tighter.

Jannik looked to Ayla. "I don't have a weapon."

"Improvise," Ayla said. She rushed toward one of the drones a moment afterward, leaping up and grabbing it by its landing struts. The drone sputtered, but then reacted by pushing higher.

Ayla held on for dear life. She towered above the pirates below as they struggled with the giant net that had entrapped them. The drone kept going skyward, and Ayla found herself above the rooftops of one of the nearby buildings.

She'd found a way out. All she had to do was survive.

Her next maneuver would be dangerous, but she couldn't fly with this drone forever. If its controllers knew what they were doing, it would lift high into the air, then cut its engines to force Ayla to plummet to her death. It didn't sound like an appealing ride.

Using her bodyweight, she rocked back and forth until she gained enough leverage to push herself forward, letting go of the drone's landing struts while hurling herself toward the rooftop nearby.

It was at least a meter drop, but it beat the alternative of falling to the streets below. Ayla caught the edge of the roof, running forward to keep herself upright on the landing. It wasn't pretty, but she managed not to lose her footing.

The drone reacted by firing another net toward her. This time, she had no way to get out of the way.

The edge of the net clamped to the ground, trapping her inside. The one below probably did similar to the pirates, but Ayla was by herself, she didn't have panicking people with her under the net. She had clarity of mind and had been in worse situations before.

The drone hovered overhead, waiting for her, making sure she was still in its sights. She didn't have to worry about it. The drone had meant to capture, not kill, programmed to arrest the citizens protesting here not to vaporize enemies. The council must have wanted to bring people to trial to make examples of them before the rest of the populace.

It meant she could safely go to work to remove the net's tethers. She grabbed her pistol once again and fired a laser blast through the holes in the net toward one of the anchors holding it down. It snapped, freeing one area.

She fired again on another anchor, and it freed a side of the net. She'd be able to get out of here without much of a problem.

Holstering the pistol again, she hit the ground and crawled out of the net. She scrambled to get onto her rear and face the drone as it would have been watching her. It didn't seem to have another net loaded and handy, so it trained another weapon on her.

Before it could fire, Ayla produced her laser pistol once more and shot a blast, hitting it in its camera receptor, causing it to spin out of control and crash like it had when she had shot the others.

Ayla let out a deep breath, content to get a few moments respite.

The pirates down below yelled and bickered with one another.

"Get us out of here Jannik!" Rams shouted.

"I'm trying. I'm trying," Jannik said.

Ayla grumbled and pushed herself to her feet. She stepped to the ledge of the rooftop and looked down.

Jannik was pulling at the base anchors of the net to no avail.

"Hey, Jannik," Ayla said.

The young pirate looked up, surprised to see Ayla on the rooftop. "I can't believe you survived that."

"Get a weapon from one of your friends and tell them to shoot out the anchors of the net. It'll release, and they can get out then."

"Ahh! Did you hear that?" Jannik turned his attention back to his companions.

Moments later, laser fire shot from under the net, whipping the edges free from the ground and releasing the pirates. The final drone flew away. Whoever was controlling it had to have understood that they would be losing their equipment if it remained there.

With the pirates out, they looked up toward Ayla.

"Are you going to stay up there?" Mihael asked.

"Yes," Ayla replied, laughing. "It's much safer up here, and if they're doing a sweep below, we'll be able to get out of the perimeter by getting to the other side of this building."

"You can't leave us," Mihael said.

Ayla sucked in her bottom lip, trying to think of what to do. She had to improvise, and Mihael was right, she wouldn't just leave them behind. She glanced back at the net, which gave her an idea. "Stand by," she said.

The net was fairly sizable, enough to be able to hold several people in place. It might just be able to reach down to where the pirates were at, and they could use it as a climbing rope to get up top. She would have to manipulate it.

"Give me a few minutes," Ayla shouted.

She got to work, slicing through the net with her laser, tying bits together so they would extend and become longer rather than wide.

Eventually, she had a makeshift rope made out of the net the drone left her. It had inadvertently been her salvation with its non-lethal weaponry.

After some time of snapping some of the rope edges, and then tying them together, Ayla determined she had a pretty good ladder. She hurled it over the side and down the building. It just about reached to the right place to where the pirates could grab on, but the shorter ones would need a little boost up.

"You expect us to climb this?" Tanya asked.

"I'm hoping Rams and maybe a couple others have enough upper body strength to get up here. There are nice handholds naturally in the netting, which should help you. After we get them up, we can tie the rope around your waist and pull you up if need be."

"That sounds like even more frightening of a prospect," Tanya said.

"Not as frightening as getting rounded up by planetary security and forced into inhaling those spores," Mihael said. "Rams, you go first since Ayla mentioned you."

Rams grumbled but reached and grabbed the top of the rope.

Ayla gripped on tight, using her body weight and the leverage of the edge of the rooftop to make sure she could keep the edge in place.

Rams ascended the building and made his way up top without much of a problem. "You're pretty smart," he said.

Ayla gave him a small smile. "Thank you."

One by one, the pirates made their way up to the rooftop via the net rope, and then Ayla pulled the rope all the way up to make sure it wasn't hanging and dangling over the ground. This way they wouldn't be able to be tracked. The pirates all assisted in hauling Tanya up along with them.

The other side of the roof was outside of the containment zone set up by the Zendan Marines. All they would have to do would be to go back down the other side and disappear into the crowds.

Mihael grabbed the edge of the net rope and tied it to some piping. "Now to repel back down," he said.

"I didn't sign up for this," Tanya said, shaking her head. "I'm supposed to be in a nice kitchen preparing meals."

"Think of it as some bonus travel," Mihael said. He tugged on the net rope and led the way, making his way down on it first, repelling off the building downward until he made it to the street. Then, he looked up at them. "See? Easy."

"Gee." Tanya rolled her eyes.

Once again, the pirates took turns making their way on the net rope, until each of them made it to the ground level. Ayla went last so she could keep watch atop the building. For now, there was no sign of any problems with anyone following them. The soldiers would have a lot on their hands dealing with so many of the protestors who still were in the streets from the sound of things.

A blast sounded, followed by a plume of smoke rising in the air. It was impossible to see anything else with the buildings in the way, but it meant another crisis would be coming soon. It seemed like the resistance had a few more of those thermal detonators left over from their display at the factory.

She couldn't worry about it. They had to get out of this zone.

"Should we head back to the spaceport?" Zahn asked. The pilot seemed eager to get back into his native habit.

"I don't think so,' Ayla said. "It'll be too suspicious. We might run into the same problems as before."

People ran down the streets as several of the protestors had made it past barricades. So far, no planetary security followed them, but it would only be a matter of time before they had the containment zone scoured. At that point, they would be hunting down stragglers on these streets.

"We have to find somewhere to hole up," Mihael said. "At least until this clears. Then we hope we can get through the spaceport."

That would be another story. Ayla had been involved in too many of these incidents. It would take a tremendous stroke of luck not to be noticed on any of their identity scans. But this planet also didn't have the most robust of security. Their years in isolation had let them get relaxed, even with their current schemes to manipulate the populace.

"We can't stand here, regardless. Let's get going." Ayla trudged forward into the city.

The streets were fairly barren, as the government had redirected traffic away from the incidents and told the populace to return to their homes. Martial law would scare a lot of people out of the streets, that was for sure.

A man came out of a building, seeming to take note of them. It was getting pretty dark out, and he looked like a mere silhouette from the distance. He stuck to the shadows, making himself more obscure.

"We're being followed," Ayla said to Mihael, keeping her voice low.

"How many?" the pirate captain asked.

"Just one."

"Let's scare him off, then."

Mihael turned a corner, motioning for the pirates to move quickly with him. Once out of sight of the prior street, he had them all line the wall, getting themselves into cover. Footsteps echoed down the empty street behind them as the man following them picked up his pace.

Their stalker rounded the corner, and Mihael stepped out to ambush him.

Ayla noted the dark features of the man in question right away. He wasn't someone working for the government, quite the contrary.

"Hervey?" Ayla asked. She was surprised to see the resistance leader out on his own.

"I thought I spotted you. The red hair is a dead giveaway," he said, pointing to Ayla's head. "I'm staying behind to direct people to another safe house we have at the outskirts of the city. Here's how you get there. And the password will be *memory hole* when you get to the door."

Ayla listened as they received their directions.

Ayla and her pirate friends settled into the safe house. It was more of a mansion situated into a side of a hill, with a sleek modern design, windows overlooking the city with what would have been breathtaking views. At least, it would have been during normal times. Today, the entire view comprised of smoke and flames, and the lights from the few buildings that hadn't been destroyed and looted. Government emergency vehicles buzzed through the thoroughfares and skyways surrounding the scene.

More than a hundred of the resistance members gathered in a large room, which was decorated with tall, fine pottery, art on the walls, and several chairs. They had a bar overlooking the city below. Several of the gathered people gazed out, but not to enjoy the view, but rather to mourn the loss of their city.

"I wish it hadn't come to this," a man said, frowning.

Hervey walked over to the man and placed a hand on his shoulder. "We didn't want this either. Remember, the council escalated with us at every turn. We tried to talk with them, to meet with them, but they refused. There's something amiss within the council, an influence I haven't been able to determine. But they're supposed to be representatives of the people, and they've done anything but work for us."

Ayla heard the conversation and scooted over toward them. "There is outside influence, and I think it might be alien in nature."

"Alien?" Hervey chuckled. "And they accuse me of being a conspiracy theorist."

"I'm serious," Ayla said. "My friends and I have been tracking the movements of one of the council members. When we found him, he kept meeting with this tall man in an environmental suit who called himself Darmarin. It didn't sound like a name but rather a race."

"I saw it myself," Mihael said. He had a drink in his hand and brushed up against Ayla's shoulder, getting a little too close for comfort, but Ayla didn't flinch.

"As wild a theory as any, but their actions also don't make sense. Why would they willfully reduce the population of this planet's brains into mush? Even if they wanted some level of control for themselves, it doesn't make sense. They have to live here, work here, with people who can't remember how to fry an egg without turning to their memory chips. It's a shame what's become of so many..." He trailed off, gazing out into the damaged cityscape beyond.

Ayla tilted her head, eyeing Hervey carefully. He seemed profoundly hurt, and she had a maternal instinct kick in to where she felt compelled to comfort him. "Did you lose someone?"

Hervey paused, the well-spoken man standing in an odd moment of awkward silence. He swallowed like he had a lump in his throat, and then cast his eyes low. "Yes. My wife. She couldn't remember anything. The time we met. Our first date. Even with the memory chip, there were holes in her mind. She became a different person. It got so bad, I eventually just left. I doubt she even remembers she was with me at this point."

Ayla hadn't had a significant other in her life that she could have truly called love. She'd been so focused on studies, and then her career in law enforcement, which led her to the agency. It had been a whirlwind of a life, which led her to some regret. Would she have been better off settling down? Those thoughts crept into the back of her head. Many men had tried to woo her, but something never felt quite right about any of the situations.

A little girl peered around the corner of a sofa then, strawberry blonde, with freckles scattered around her fair features, and about the bluest eyes Ayla had ever seen. She seemed nervous around all of the strangers, but then rushed to Hervey's leg, wrapping her arms around the resistance leader and holding him tightly.

Hervey placed a hand on the little girl's shoulder. "It's okay, Miranda Jane. These are friends."

It must have been even harder to lose the mother of one's daughter. Ayla couldn't comprehend what Hervey had gone through, but her heart twisted at the thought, nonetheless.

"I'm sorry for your loss," she managed to say, not sure how else to speak of the conversation. Hervey seemed like a good man from the brief interactions she'd had with him—competent at the very least. He didn't deserve to lose someone to the memory loss induced by the spore. It seemed it was worse in some people than others, a truly insidious side-effect.

"It drives me to make sure this never happens to anyone else," Hervey said, turning his attention outward to the skyline and the smoke and flames that encapsulated the city. He squeezed Miranda closer to him. "We still have a lot of work to do."

"We do," Ayla agreed. "And I think the first order of business should be tracking this Darmarin." She glanced toward Mihael, who seemed to have found delight in the bar, helping himself to another drink. The pirate captain had his weakness, but he noted Ayla's glance all the same, topped off his glass with an amber liquid, and sauntered over to her.

"You weren't talking about me, were you?" he asked with a soft smile.

"No," Ayla said flatly, noting an instant disappointment in the pirate's eyes. "But I was about to call you over anyway. We have a tracer on the Darmarin, right?"

While they spoke, Hervey crouched down to the little girl and told her to run along. She complied with her father's wishes, skipping away from the gathered resistance members.

"As far as I know, unless they've discovered it during all the chaos."

"We need to get back to our ship to triangulate the signal," Ayla said, frowning. "But being there was how we got stuck in this mess to begin with. We weren't authorized to launch. They hit us with planetary defenses. It forced us to land, and then the floodgates opened on these riots."

Hervey listened with interest, and then brought his fingers to his temple, pressing his fingers against it. "I've got a terrible headache. Too much stimulation, I think. Though I think I might have some good news for you."

"What's that?" Ayla asked.

"Our society has problems, which can be a benefit in this situation. If there was an order to keep anyone grounded, you'll just have to wait a few days, and the government and people won't have the history in their memory banks anymore. We'll ensure through our networks that there's another crisis for the council to be focusing on, and this will fade into their memory chips. Everything is a fleeting moment. It means we're not very good at manhunts. We also don't have persistent trouble because of it. They're not counting on a group of us rebelling without having taken the spore. My people will also get you a new ship ident codes so when you return to the spaceport, you can trick the operators into think you're someone else."

"Codes will work that easily?" Mihael asked, cocking a brow.

"I'd bet on it. But like I said, stay here until it's safe. Relax. Recover. Martial law will fizzle, and we'll slowly go back to normal here. These crises can only be amped up until the people have forgotten about it."

Ayla considered how such a society could function, or not function as it might be in some instances. It was frightening. Hervey knew what he was talking about here, though. They were in his domain, and so she would take his tactical advice, so long as the pirates would agree to it.

"Okay. We'll wait here for a few days and see what happens," Ayla said.

Hervey nodded. "This is why I'm confident we can be in a safe house and not be discovered. Our resistance has been planning on making our move for a while, but we need to figure out the next steps."

"You've done well to slow the production of the immortality spore," Ayla said. "It'll buy more time for the Imperial Space Marines to get here."

Hervey shifted, his eyes drifting outward again.

"Something I said?" Ayla asked.

"Our world's been free from the Imperium's influence a long time. It's been forgotten. Part of what our resistance here is about is having our own freedom. I'm not sure I want to have an army of outsiders arrive and restore order."

Ayla hadn't considered that this resistance might not be friendly to the Imperium. Had she backed the wrong horse? No, what the government here was doing was illegal. She knew that she might come to odds with Hervey and the others once the space Marines arrived. And she had meant to defer any conflict until then. She still would, because getting into an ideological war wouldn't accomplish anything. It wasn't as if she could form a local government loyal to the Imperium right now. Fighting with Hervey over the future would be something for another time.

"You value freedom," Ayla said. "It's a very human trait. Something we've all enjoyed in the Imperium for as long we've had Pax Terra." She spoke of the period ever since the last Great War, hundreds of years ago. The one that had resulted in the obliteration of humanity's original home of Earth, and their reestablishment of a new home on Terra Prime. It was a dark time for the species, one that they had hopefully learned their lesson in regard to and wouldn't endure again.

Empires only lasted so long, but she hoped that the Imperium wouldn't begin to fray under her watch. It was her job to keep it together after all.

"Anyway, we've got a few days as you said. Why don't we all relax and think about other matters. What are your hobbies outside of overthrowing planetary governments?" She tried to smile her brightest and give a twinkle in her eye that she knew could make men forget any sort of conflict. It helped being a woman in these situations.

Mihael didn't seem to like the way she looked at Hervey, judging from his expression, but he wouldn't pick a fight here and now. All they had to do would be to wait things out and maintain the peace.

Easy enough.

"I enjoy aerial drone racing," Hervey said. "Not the kind that's computer-controlled, but with a real pilot working the controls."

Zahn stepped forward once the conversation turned to piloting. "I did a little bit of that myself. Fun stuff. Not like being inside a vessel and flying personally, but it's still exhilarating. I once crashed a drone into a corporate big wig's flier. It was a bad day, let me tell you…"

The talk of politics died down for the evening.

28

Ayla and the pirates waited three more days in the posh mansion. It made sense for the resistance to have such an elaborate set up. If they didn't have access to finances, they wouldn't have made it very far in their attempted subversion of the local government.

Hervey gave her a room with a bed, a nice set up compared to her recent life with the pirates in a small bunk. Though it wasn't home, and she longed to be back on Terra Prime, she'd been in far worse accommodations on recent missions.

Just as the resistance leader predicted, the local government broadcasts started as a stern warning toward Zenda's inhabitants, and then quickly devolved back into normalcy. Several of the resistance members from the protest had been rounded up, given the spore, and newscasters said they had been "humanely rehabilitated."

It meant their memories had been wiped, and these people were now going to live as mindless drones controlled by their chips. Apparently, the council determined they had captured most of those involved, and that whatever remained of the rebellion wouldn't be a threat.

At the same time, Hervey's resistance still had their memories, and they plotted next steps. Some wanted to storm the council's chambers, but several in the room also felt the governmental pacification over the last few days was meant to lull the spored population into a sense of security, and that any action on their part would be met with a defensive trap from local forces.

It was a good theory, Ayla had to admit. She encouraged the resistance to be vigilant and to wait for assistance from the Imperial Space Marines. With the spore facility destroyed, they didn't have to make any quick moves that could put their health in jeopardy. The government would be there, and the greater Imperium already would have found them to be rebellious and treasonous to help their cause.

Hervey didn't seem to like this plan, still advocating for freedom and an independent Zenda to result from this conflict, but he managed to keep his idealistic fervor from reaching a boiling point. The logic of the situation at hand being one in which he would lose far less members of his budding resistances' lives if they didn't oppose the Imperium.

Ayla's focus would be more on this Darmarin, or Darmarins? She wasn't sure as to how the group thought of the plural of the alien name. The pirates still had the tracer on the suit, and she wanted to get back into action to find out where the individual had gone off world. No news over the last few days had confirmed any machinations by non-human groups.

If the Darmarin were aliens and did want to stay in hiding to try to erode the Imperium, they did a good job of it. Regardless, soon, she would be on the move to root out the cause of this dastardly local political hotbed of a situation.

Regardless, Ayla needed to determine whether the Darmarin were aliens first, and if they still lingered around this planet. To do that, they would have to return to the *Peregrine*. She'd been itching for action for days, but also had the good sense to have the patience to wait out this local Zendan government so they could move onto other plans. It seemed to have worked.

She entered the main gathering room overlooking the Zendan

capital. Over the past several days, the fires had been put out, the smoke cleared. The city looked like it had returned to normal. From this distance, one could hardly see any remnants of the protest from a few days prior. The facility they'd destroyed was obscured by skyscrapers.

Life returned to normal. The people with memory chip implants likely would never even be aware there were problems. They'd return right to their lives, working for the benefit of this corrupt local government.

The thought sent chills up Ayla's spine. They had almost gotten her infected with the immortality spore. What would her life have been like if they had succeeded? Would she forget the Imperium? Jorus? Her new pirate friends? Her entire life's work wouldn't be remembered. They probably would have put her into some desk job where she wouldn't leave the planet again.

It made her empathize for Hervey's situation all the more. Losing a loved one to such an insidious scheme must have been immensely painful. Even though she didn't agree with his emphasis on total freedom for the inhabitants of Zenda, she had to admire his determination to work hard for what he believed in. With such difficult circumstances, it took a very strong man to do what he did.

The room remained empty for Ayla to collect her thoughts. She hated the waiting games in this profession. Now, she waited both to make her own move and for the space Marines to arrive. But she'd be able to act soon. All she had to do was wait for the pirates to wake up and get going—something, which might take hours with the amount of alcohol they had bee ingesting over the last few days of their wait.

Jannik was the first to arrive, stretching his lanky arms up over his head and giving Ayla a smile. "You're up bright and early," he said.

"Preparing myself for our departure. I hope Hervey's right and the council will be too busy to notice us slipping through their cracks."

"I've done some research overnight. I saw nothing about our ships or us on the local nets," Jannik said. "With the spaceport getting overrun the way it was, I think a lot of the records got lost in the fray. We got out without so much as a scratch."

"Don't count your chickens," Ayla said with a chuckle. "Still, I'm impressed. A cargo operator doing recon work on the nets? Unexpected."

"I don't plan on being a cargo operator forever," Jannik said, glancing out the windows toward the cityscape.

He was young and had his dreams. Ayla envied being his age, even though she didn't have too many more years on him. With everything she'd seen, however, she'd matured beyond the pirates, Mihael included. When was the last time she had a real dream or aspiration of her own beyond doing her job faithfully and returning to her gardens to relax?

Her current work mattered and meant something. Every time she went out to protect the Imperium, she saved lives. How could she ask for anything beyond that? It also presented thrills and adrenaline like nothing else, even in her prior work in planetary law enforcement. She figured she should count herself as blessed.

"Good for you. We'll have to get off this planet safely before we get to whatever else it is you plan on doing," Ayla said.

Tanya entered the room next, swaying her hips a little more than usual. Right behind her was Zahn, and Ayla could see why Tanya had such a swagger to her by the way the pilot looked at her. Interesting. She hadn't noticed any relationship between the pilot and the chef prior to this day, but she'd been preoccupied in her duties.

Rams appeared from a lavatory doorway, and then Mihael made his way out of the room, looking a little disheveled. He must have had a hard night of drinking once more.

"Looks like everyone's here," Ayla said brightly.

Mihael rubbed his temples. "Here is a relative term."

"Technically, with the way a planet orbits a sun, here isn't even here from one moment to the next," Zahn said.

"I'm too hungover to think about physics," Mihael said.

"Hopefully not too hungover to get to the spaceport and see if we can find where this Darmarin went," Ayla said.

"I'll be fine after a stim hypo and some water," Mihael said.

"Good." Ayla glanced at the assembled team. It might not have been who she would have picked for an Imperial mission, but she felt good about her prospects because these people cared and worked together well as a unit. They'd survived quite a strange adventure so far. "Let's get going, then. We don't want to give whoever this is more time to hatch new plans on this populace, or the populace of other worlds for that matter."

The pirates grunted their agreements, ready to follow Ayla. Even though Mihael had final say, they'd done well falling into line behind her lead over these past few days. Getting them extracted from the barricaded zone in the city had helped with their confidence in her.

The group broke to gather the meager belongings they'd brought with them, and Ayla and Mihael went to say their goodbyes to Hervey.

"Don't make this too much of a farewell," Hervey said. "I expect you to be back here soon enough. We're going to need your help to formally overthrow the council."

"Count on it," Ayla said, slinging a pack over her shoulder. "Let's get going, then."

They parted with the resistance leaders, hitching a ride from some of Hervey's surrogates in a small flitter that took them to the spaceport.

The damage at the spaceport was hard to miss. The fence had fallen, the main building had several windows blown out, and much of the furniture inside removed, but people and bots manned the place just as they had before. The workers acted as if nothing had happened.

It made for an eerie feeling as Ayla passed through with the others. Mihael took point, seeming to have recovered over the last several minutes from his prior night's bender, making his way to a counter where a woman stood.

He spoke with the woman for a time, out of earshot of the others, and then returned to them, shaking his head.

"What's wrong?" Ayla asked.

"Nothing. That's what bothers me. It was too easy."

"The power of forgetting."

Mihael shrugged and motioned the others to follow him.

Soon enough, they'd made their way back out to the landing pad where the *Peregrine* still remained. The rioters hadn't torn apart the ship, nor had they been able to get in thanks to the security codes only the pirates possessed. The ship looked no worse for the wear, other than the places where the planetary defenses had connected with a blast on the hull, leaving a scorched markings among the painted metal.

Mihael input his codes, lowering the ramp so they could board. He stood for a long moment, breathing a deep sigh of relief. "It's nice to be back. Felt like I might never get to fly her again."

"I miss my own ship," Ayla said. And she did. The flier the Imperium had provided her with had access to all kinds of tricks and gadgets she found helpful on covert missions, as well as a top of the line artificial intelligence, which gave her instant access to the entirety of the imperial databanks, along with a smart search function she could use to research aspects of her cases without her having to expend the time or energy. She would have liked to have learned more about the Imperium's history with any Darmarin but, for now, she had to fly in blind.

The pirate crew made their way to their respective stations on the ship, with Mihael, Rams, Zahn, and Ayla heading to the bridge. They stopped there, and Zahn began his pre-flight preparations, booting up the computer and getting the engines going.

The pilot tapped in the commands to communicate with spaceport control. He'd been given new ident codes for their ship from Hervey's people. Ayla sucked in her lower lip, nervous about how well those would work.

The console chirped. "We have clearance to take off this time," Zahn said.

"Small blessings," Mihael said, settling into his captain's chair. "Question is, where are we going?"

Rams worked at the security console, furrowing his brow as he looked at the information. "We've got the same link into the asteroid field. Whoever this fellow is has parked there for a long while."

"That means he's taken a heavy interest in the planet and needs a secret base of operations," Ayla said.

"Pirate tactics," Mihael said. "Well, if there's one thing we know, it's those. Which means we should be able to defeat them. Zahn, lift us off and set course for that asteroid field."

The *Peregrine* shot into the sky.

29

WHEN THEY ARRIVED IN THE ASTEROID FIELD, ZAHN WENT TO WORK. His hands moved rapidly at the controls, dodging all of the space debris as best he could to ensure the *Peregrine* didn't meet a demise by running into a large rock to slice through its hull.

Ayla didn't envy the pilot and would have automated the job with the AI controls if she had been on her ship. Flying still required a human touch in some places, though, and Zahn did his job with expert precision.

They converged upon the signal, which came from a large planetoid in the middle of the field. The planetoid had some gaseous atmosphere to it, swirling with a vomit-green coloration which looked rather unappealing to breathe. They would need environmental suits to go down there, or so it appeared.

Rams scanned the planetoid. "There's a pocket of oxygen atmosphere on one section of the planetoid. It's not the cleanest, but it is breathable."

"I think I'll suit up just the same," Ayla said.

"What are we expecting to find down there?" Mihael asked. "I'm not sure I want to risk the crew to go into some thick green fog."

"Then don't," Ayla said.

Mihael looked toward her skeptically.

"I'll go alone," Ayla said.

"You can't do that," Mihael protested, standing from the captain's chair to face her.

"Of course, I can. I've done it before." Ayla crossed her arms. "I'm an agent of the Imperium. This is a government mission. Honestly, there's no need for any of you to put yourselves in danger. You've done far more than enough already. Besides, if these Darmarin have some kind of spacebar defenses, you'll need to maneuver the *Peregrine* long enough to get me a ride out of here. With Zahn at the helm and Rams on weapons, it'll be better. Tanya and Jannik won't be able to help me, and you're the captain who should stay with your ship."

Mihael opened his mouth to further fight for the matter, clearly desiring to protect Ayla, but he closed it again. The pirate captain had to know she was right. This would be the most effective way to go get information. "I don't like it."

"It's fine," Ayla said, stepping toward him and placing a hand on his shoulder. "It'll be easier to be stealthy alone anyway. One person can sneak around where a group can't. It's how I've gotten this far in life."

Mihael locked eyes with her, gazing at her with an intensity he hadn't shown before. He cared. A little too much, perhaps, but it was genuine. "Be careful out there."

"I will. Someone has to report back to the emperor." Ayla gave a soft smile, stepping back.

Mihael waved her away and resumed his seat.

Ayla made her way back into the ship's bowels, veering toward her quarters to pick up some of her gear and change. She took her time getting into the suit, careful to be sure all of the vacuum seals were airtight. Once the environment suit was on, she turned on the air filtration system, which pumped in oxygen and circulated cooling through the suit to maintain air temperature. For the moment, she kept her helmet off and made her way back to the cargo bay where Jannik stood ready to man the controls.

"You're going to dive out of the cargo bay?" Jannik asked. He sounded wary.

"That's the plan. Don't worry. I know how to use jetpack controls. This isn't my first hyperspace race."

"Good luck," Jannik said, heading back to the control area and engaging a forcefield to make sure his zone remained pressurized when he opened the doors.

Ayla secured her helmet, which then made a *whoosh* sound when it pressurized. The holo-dash displayed her air pressure and remaining oxygen, as well as the temperature. All looked good and showed no signs of problems. Her laser pistol was secure in the holster at her side, locked in for her descent.

She then moved over to the jetpack, leaning over to slip the straps over her back. It was heavy, but she'd handled the equipment before. The pack attached itself to Ayla's environment suit, powering up and coming online a moment later. The holo-dash added a jetpack fuel rate as well as a speedometer.

She gave a thumbs up to Jannik, ready to go. With the suit, she could hear her breathing.

"Mihael to Ayla," came the pirate's voice through her suit comm.

"Radio contact established. Everything is a go." Ayla took a deep breath. Even with the maglocks on the boots and the suit on her, the depressurization sensation could be uncomfortable.

Jannik turned the bay lights red, which flashed with warning as the air was about to exit the room. Ayla couldn't feel it, but the environmental controls had shifted to create the vacuum.

The doors opened out into space, a strange swirl of stars in the background and thin gas from the planetoid creating bright white and green colors all around her. She couldn't call the gaseous colors beautiful, but it was a novel visual experience.

The *Peregrine* had gotten close enough that there was a mild amount of atmosphere, not a complete depressurization like she would have experienced in space. It made her move a little bit easier as Ayla detached her maglocks and dove out of the cargo bay.

Gravity pulled her downward toward the asteroid surface at incredible speeds, but Ayla engaged her jetpack to counter the descent, slowing her fall to a reasonable pace. Soon, she stabilized into the lower atmosphere, able to see formations of jagged black rock material all around her. The sky still had a green hue to it, but there was an area where it had the pocket of breathable atmosphere from before, which seemed to have cleaner air than everyone else. There had to have been a forcefield surrounding it.

As she came closer, Ayla spotted a protrusion from the ground, a spider-like design of a metallic structure blending into the rock face. It had some lighting to it, which would allow small ships to land within the area safely,

Ayla set herself down a safe distance away from the structure. Lights blinked, but everything appeared to be quiet outside of their enclosed atmosphere. First, she had to determine whether it was a soft field that would allow matter through but maintain the atmosphere, or if she would have to find some other way around and inside. It would be easy to determine, all she had to do was test it.

She picked a small stone off the ground, which fit in her hand, and she tossed it. The stone hit the field but shimmered through it rather than hitting the field like a wall. It was a good sign, the field designed to let objects through rather than to keep them out.

With the field tested, Ayla stepped through it. Her environment suit made it so she couldn't feel any of the tingling that would have been caused from the electrical elements of such a field, allowing her safely inside. So far, this trip had been no problem.

Though she remained outside of the structure that appeared to be some kind of entrance into an underground facility. The flitter landing pad was off to her left as she circled the structure, looking for a hatch or a doorway where she might gain entrance.

Eventually, she found one, a large doorway big enough for a small vehicle to enter to deliver cargo. It had an electronic pad to the side allowing access. The only problem was, if she input her access, it would alert whoever was here to her presence.

She guessed they wouldn't be friendly.

But it wouldn't have been the first time Ayla had to pick a lock. She set her jetpack off to the side. Even in a low gravity environment like this, she would prefer not to carry such heavy equipment. Then, Ayla depressurized her suit.

As the pirates had told her, the atmosphere was breathable. At least, she didn't faint within moments of inhaling the air. It had a rotten smell to it, however, some of the exterior gasses mixing with the air. She wouldn't want to breathe this for too long, but she needed her hands outside of her environmental suit in order to perform the fine work on the locking mechanism.

Ayla removed the suit's gloves, and then produced a small tool kit from the suit. With it, she disassembled the electronic pad, revealing a host of microchips and wiring behind it. There was a port that allowed her to plug in her environmental suit's onboard computer and interface with it.

The mechanism had standard coding, which made this matter easy. All she had to do was enter the Imperial codes all manufacturers had to comply with, and it would give her access.

Her onboard computer chirped at her as it connected with the door's input, and all looked like it was going to plan. For a moment, nothing happened. Ayla looked up at the door, wondering if it had some kind of malfunction. But then the door creaked, making a shrill sound as it forced itself open, the metal having a lack of lubrication. Rust shed off its sides, either a product of the environment on this surface or from age.

The corridor inside was dimly lit, with concrete floors and large piping along the sides. Steam shot out from one of the pipes, which stopped after a few moments. It made the already hazy air more difficult to see through.

Ayla stepped inside, returning her helmet to its place so she could use its night vision functions. She also slipped her glove back on, figuring she might as well pressurize her suit and get herself some clean air without the sulfurous smell. It was a relief once the suit started to circulate the oxygen, which Ayla breathed in deeply.

The piping led down to what appeared to be an open lift, a standard mining extraction set up on this asteroid. This place must have supplied metals for Zenda and been forgotten over the years, from the look of the dingy place with a lack of maintenance.

If the Darmarin were here, Ayla could see no sign of them. They must have embedded themselves in lower levels. It felt a lot like a trap, but it was one Ayla had to walk into if she wanted to uncover the mystery of what went on here.

She stepped forward, her footfalls sticking through each step, the atmosphere causing some light adhesion, enough to be irritating, but not enough to slow her down. Something dripped from the pipes, which beat onto other pipes and echoed through the room rhythmically. A crashing sound could be heard from farther below. Something was down there.

Ayla made it to the lift and depressed the button to go down a level. Her heart raced despite herself. She'd been in situations like this several times, but it always rattled her nerves. She had to be able to react quickly if something went awry.

The lift stopped with a jolt, revealing another dimly lit path through some rock face. She'd descended into these mines. Something clicked up ahead, machinery. Was it still in operation? There would be only one way to find out.

She stepped forward, the pathway turning around some of the rocks, until she found the source of the clicking.

Several bots blocked the corridor in front of her. Some had spidery legs, others were on treads, with a couple of drones flying as well. They trained their laser sights on her.

Ayla backpedaled, realizing she'd stumbled her way into a small army. They'd been waiting for her to come down, and she was all alone.

It would take too much time to get back into the lift and ascend to the surface. They would open fire, especially since the lift had no doors to close and protect her. She would have to make her stand here.

Ayla drew her laser pistol, ready for the bots to make their way around the corner and open fire on her.

30

LASERS SHOT TOWARD AYLA. SHE DODGED THE FIRST VOLLEY FROM THE bots coming around the corner and pointed her laser pistol back to return fire. The blasts hit one of the metallic monstrosities but did little to damage it.

She had nowhere to run, nowhere to take cover. This was the worst of all possible situations. The place had looked vacant excepting for the noises she'd heard in lower levels, and so she couldn't have thought the security in this place would be so robust.

One or two bots, she would have been able to handle, but this many?

The drones buzzed around the next bend first. Ayla reached up to fire a direct shot on one of its cameras, but the second managed to counterattack, nearly hitting Ayla in the hip. The laser shot blasted rock off the wall beside her, which ricocheted to hit her in the side.

Ayla winced. It would bruise later, but she still had all of these bots to deal with and couldn't stop to deal with her pain. If only she had been able to get a few of those thermal explosives from the resistance, she would have been able to do something more. Unlike most of her missions, she was woefully ill-prepared with her simple laser pistol, and the holdout pistol and knife she stored in her boot.

Those small weapons wouldn't do her much good.

More laser shots trailed after her. She wouldn't be able to evade the bots much longer.

Then, a solution dawned on her. She could make her own explosive.

Running toward the lift, Ayla flipped switches to set her laser pistol to overload. She could make it explode and use it as a grenade, so long as she managed to stay out of the way of the bots while it charged.

Ayla ran back into the lift cab, the open area leaving her exposed, however, there was a small lip behind the rock face where the cab opened and allowed her some semblance of safety. It would only last a moment, the bots firing their lasers into the cab, rattling the lift while she waited for her laser pistol to heat.

Her weapon buzzed, on the precipice of exploding, and Ayla reached her arm out to toss the pistol in the direction of the bots. It skidded across the gravelly ground, clanking against one of the legs of the bots.

The security bots were only programmed to do one thing—kill the intruder, not worrying about keeping themselves safe. Their limited algorithmic processors would only see a dead weapon being sent their away, regardless.

They maintained their fire, making it impossible for Ayla to get out of her small spot of cover. She held her breath, not wanting to even have the rise and fall of her chest expose any of her to the bots' attacks.

The laser pistol overloaded, resulting in the crackle of electrical fire and a small explosion just out of Ayla's line of sight. The laser fire stopped, giving Ayla a moment of respite to look out beyond and see what was going on.

Dust and smoke obscured her vision at first, but her helmet filtered the air and switched to a different spectrum to allow Ayla to get a good luck. A bunch of scrap metal rested where the bots had been, with some of the ceiling of the corridor having caved in atop them. However, the single flying drone lingered in the background. It spotted her.

The drone opened fire on her, this shot piercing through her suit and hitting her left shoulder. The blast stung her like she had pressed it against a hot stove. Ayla didn't even want to look to see how bad the burn would be. The pain ran down her arm and made her scream.

The release of energy helped enough for Ayla to recalibrate and get back behind cover. She cradled her shoulder with her right hand, wincing.

Her gambit had given her a fighting chance, but she wasn't out of the woods yet. She still had this bot to deal with. Willing herself to ignore the pain, Ayla reached to her boot to grab her holdout pistol.

It was small, and packed less of a punch, but it would do the trick if she could aim true.

The drone buzzed into the cab, spinning as it tracked Ayla to her small place of cover.

Ayla dove to the side as more laser fire came in her direction. When she did, she landed on her left shoulder.

Fortunately, she was ambidextrous, and she held the pistol up in her right hand, steadied by the ground, her elbow pressed against the gravel. She opened fire on the drone, hitting it.

The laser fire was too weak to blast this one apart easily. It turned toward her once more.

She had to make her stand now. She was on the ground, injured, and wouldn't be able to keep up with the movements of this drone.

Ayla fired again, holding down the trigger so a long beam would continuously hit the bot.

This time, the glass exploded on the drone, causing it to lose its place in the air and smash against the wall.

Ayla pushed herself into a seated position, leaning against the rock beside her. She'd managed to survive an onslaught of security bots against the odds. But she had taken her licks as well. Her shoulder throbbed as her adrenaline wore off. What she wouldn't have given for a numbing agent or painkiller.

But she didn't have one. All she had now was a small weapon. The most important thing she could do would be to patch the place where her shoulder had taken the injury so she could escape from this place again once she needed to leave.

Ayla pulled out a patch kit from one of the pouches on the suit, securing it into place and allowing the adhesive to stick. The suit pressurized, the air flowing inside. A small consolation for the pain in her shoulder rubbing against the suit's interior lining.

All she had left for weapons was her small holdout pistol and her knife. Not exactly the ideal situation for her to be deep within a mine controlled by some enemy force. Ideally, she would have had some recon team work with her but, for now, she only had herself, and she had to get to the bottom of what this Darmarin was up to before it made another move on the Zendan population.

With the spore production facility out of commission, it bought her some time, unless the council decided to move forward with other plans. What did they want a dumbed down population for, anyway? Would they be making some move to export these people and control them around the galaxy?

It seemed like a foolish idea, but she had heard they meant to replicate this on other worlds. And if the spore had gotten out, if the pirates had succeeded in their original mission to export the substance, the entire Terran Imperium could have been in danger.

She supposed it was a long game with these Darmarin, but to what end, she still couldn't say. Hopefully, as she made her way deeper into their base of operations, she would be able to uncover some information the Imperium could use.

After checking her pressurization again, making sure the suit functioned, Ayla stood and surveyed her surroundings.

The small army of bots sent after her were thoroughly dispatched. It didn't mean she would be completely out of danger, however. In all likelihood, there would be more security features guarding whatever lay in wait in the depths of this asteroid.

Ayla proceeded back down the path which had been cut into the rock by miners. It wound and descended deeper into the center of the asteroid, where the most valuable ore would have been located for extraction.

There, she found a flat patch where several crates of supplies and mining equipment had been stashed. The Darmarin hadn't bothered to put any lighting into this place, giving a creepy air to the mine. Her suit's light cast shadows, keeping Ayla on edge as everything seemed to move and watch her.

She continued on ahead toward another sealed doorway. This one designed for a human-sized person to step through. It had the same access pad as the one she had encountered on the exterior of the asteroid, which she used the same tactics to bypass the security systems as she had before.

This time, the security pad blinked red. Something had triggered within the system. Perhaps it had been keyed to stop her imperial access codes from working. Whoever was here learned from her original tampering.

Two lasers popped out from the rock face, training on her. They opened fire.

Ayla backpedaled, the laser bolts hitting the ground in front of her. The security system tracked her, the laser sights following her with red dots tracking their aim.

She managed to get behind some of the crates before the system fired again. It wouldn't be easy to get past this portion of the security system.

A bioroid bot on treads appeared, making matters worse. It circled around to her side of the crates, making it unsafe to remain in her cover. The bioroid had fork arms, which spun at a rapid pace—a mining bot meant to drill into rock. Those things would cut through her suit and flesh far more easily if it came too close.

The bioroid pressed forward. Ayla dodged. When she did so, it triggered the doorway security lasers to fire again.

She wouldn't be able to keep evading the lasers while keeping out of the way of the bioroid. Eventually, one of them would catch up to her.

Ayla decided to play chicken with the bioroid standing near to one of the crates. If she could time it right...

The bioroid spun and wheeled toward her, like it intended to ram her through with its fork arms. Ayla dodged out of the way, letting it crash into one of the containers. Its drill bits carved through the crate's metal surface, sparking about.

The bot pulled backward, near Ayla. She stopped and lingered for a dangerous second while it approached.

The security system opened fire. Ayla stepped out of the way to allow the lasers to pelt into the bot. The bot shook and convulsed as it was hit, the lasers shorting out its systems. Its arms stopped spinning, and it stopped moving on its treads.

It smoked, leaving her with the laser system ahead to handle.

Ayla moved toward the bioroid, eyeing its processing core. If she could get the bot going again without it having its programming to kill her, she might be able to utilize it. Ayla opened its back compartment and scanned the wiring inside.

She wasn't an engineer by any means, but she had seen enough of these machines to know that some of their motor functions were separated from their main processing cores. The processors gave the commands, but the arms and treads could operate independently.

She jacked in with her suit's computer, trying to see if she could make heads or tails of the system. Fortunately, the bioroid didn't have too complex of programming, which made sense as it would have been operated by miners who weren't typically the savviest with technology.

She turned on the motor functions and the drill bit arms. Then, she set the bioroid to move forward, with its drills spinning at rapid speeds.

As it moved toward the door, the laser systems ignored the bot. As Ayla suspected, the lasers were programmed to detect life and go after it, leaving the machines alone.

The bioroid slammed into the sealed door, and its drill bits began to work, punching a hole through it. Soon enough, the doorway had a big hole in it from a collapsed paneling, the bioroid continuing on its programming from Ayla and pressing ahead inside to whatever lay behind the door.

Ayla gathered her courage and ran forward, able to outpace the red dot tracking sensors of the lasers. She dove though the small opening the bioroid made and rolled into the other side.

There, Ayla looked up to see a big control center with several screens monitoring various areas of the asteroid, interior and exterior. The control center had a robust computer terminal big enough to have three people stationed. Only no humans were present inside.

Instead, one creature stood there, tall and lanky, looking almost like a mantis in the way it held itself. Its ribs could be seen, and it looked like it wore or had some kind of shell of armor over its shoulders. Its head had spikes to it, and its arms were very long. This was an alien life, perhaps the first humanity had ever come across.

She had found her Darmarin.

31

<hr>

THE CREATURE DIDN'T LOOK AS DAUNTING AS AYLA WOULD HAVE expected from an alien. Sure, it had its features that looked foreign, like a mixture of bug and lizard but standing upright as a man. It had a height advantage over her, and its exoskeletal-armored appearance, but by the same token, the Darmarin had a fragile quality to it. The creature wasn't muscular but lanky and skinny.

Ayla had no concept of how life might work on other worlds, it wasn't her specialty. She dealt with very human problems of criminals and rebellions against the Imperium, but she had to imagine this creature came from a world with lower gravity than Terra Prime, one where muscular features wouldn't have mattered too much.

Even though its overall appearance didn't instill fear in her, when the Darmarin cast its eyes upon her, Ayla froze.

The Darmarin's eyes shone black, soulless, like the depths of space. Whereas the physical appearance of the creature overall didn't intimidate her, those orbs cast a demonic stare. There wasn't kindness or compassion there, but the creature's piercing gaze had the quality of a wild animal in self-preservation mode. Fight or flight.

"You passed through my security," the Darmarin said. Without the voice-filter in its suit, the vocal cords sounded grainy, between a growl and a whisper.

"I did," Ayla said, clutching her holdout pistol more tightly and pointing it in the alien's direction. "Who are you? What do you want with us?"

The creature surveyed her coolly. "If I spoke of such matters, I would be betraying my people. I cannot do that, no more than you could with yours. Though, thankfully for us, not all your species has that compunction. A violent and strange breed humans are."

"We do what we must to survive," Ayla said.

"As do we," the Darmarin replied. The way he spoke the words was threatening. There would be no negotiating here, no dialing this down. These creatures had set their plans in motion, and it was clear to Ayla that the Darmarin meant harm to humanity.

It made sense as she put the pieces together. Erase memories, erase aging, one created a docile populace. At that point, the aliens could do what they wanted with humans. Ayla could only imagine the endgame. Would they have been like lambs led to slaughter? Would the aliens have used humanity as slaves? Neither option sounded like an appealing end to the Imperium nor the human race.

She wanted to bring in this creature alive. The interrogators at the agency would have a field day with this creature. So would the bio-scientists, but her priority here would be to get out alive first. If she didn't, all of her information would be lost on this creature. The emperor might never know of a threat to mankind.

The Darmarin moved with incredible speed. Its lack of muscular nature made it light on its feet, or rather on points at the end of knife-like legs. The points *clacked* on the ground, giving Ayla warning of what would be coming toward her.

Ayla fired her laser pistol. The blast hit the Darmarin square in the chest, stopping its forward rush.

However, when the laser bolt faded, no burn marks remained. It was as if the laser blast simply evaporated on it, with a small amount of steam rising from where Ayla had shot.

This wasn't good at all. Ayla took a few steps backward.

"You'll find I am impervious to your human weapons. How your species is harmed by mere concentrated light I cannot fathom. We absorb the energy. It makes us stronger."

It was like some kind of photosynthesis on steroids, Ayla surmised, since laser blasts could burn plants into ash as surely as they could a human, in her experience. Either way, she didn't want to get into a hand-to-hand tangle with this creature. She couldn't imagine it going well. She had no idea where its weak points were. It had scales and armor instead of flesh. Her knife would do little good in this fight.

She'd found what she had come here for, confirmation that alien life existed, and that they were hostile toward humanity. It would have to be enough, as much as she wanted to scour the computer banks of this asteroid and find out if the Darmarin had other plans they were hatching upon humanity.

More information couldn't be worth the cost of her life, and so she took off running back toward the door where the bioroid and blown a hole in to allow her entry.

The Darmarin moved with incredible speed. Before she reached the aperture, she found her nemesis standing in her way. The creature took a swipe at her with its long hands. Even though it didn't have much muscle mass to its swing, it managed to connect with her helmet, and its fingertips were sharp, shattering the frontal glass of her environmental suit.

The stench of the atmosphere flooded her suit, causing Ayla to gag. It was breathable air, she remembered that much, but the surprise of the foul smell slowed her down just enough for the Darmarin to take another swing at her with its other arm. It rotated with a long, falling motion to gain momentum, but it was effective.

This time, the Darmarin smashed her helmet into pieces, leaving Ayla's head exposed.

She had to close her eyes to prevent the transparent material from getting into them and blinding her. When she opened them again, she found herself flat on her back with the Darmarin standing over her.

It pressed its pincer leg to her chest. From the way its fingers tore right through her helmet, Ayla knew that if the Darmarin pushed its leg point through her suit, she would be a dead woman.

"I commend your tenacity for getting this far. By my calculations, you should have never gotten past my bots and the laser defenses, but you managed. Just as you managed to slow our plans using the spores on the populace of the planet. But it will not matter. You will be dead soon, and we will continue with only a slight setback. It would be better if there were a way to have a human deliver a message we should not be trifled with but, for now, it is our will to remain unknown to human minds."

Ayla wasn't sure what came over her, but she found this alien to be nasty in its casual cruelty and disregard for life. It was everything the Imperium stood against, and she wasn't about to let this creature destroy her and burrow back into its little hole to hatch new plans. Unable to physically get out of the way of the Darmarin, all Ayla could do was spit at the creature, making it clear humanity wouldn't go down without resistance.

The spit landed on the Darmarin's leg, and the creature recoiled in pain. Its leg-point tore into Ayla's suit, but it pulled away and didn't strike at her insides. She scrambled to a seated position, crab-crawling backward to get some distance between her and the alien.

What had just happened here? It looked like the spit had hurt the Darmarin, doing more than her holdout laser pistol had for her self-defense. What properties could spit have that could bother such a creature?

Ayla realized that the very property which keep humans alive might have been detrimental to these aliens. What if that was why the Darmarin wore the environmental suit, not just to hide its identity, but to evade humidity in the air of human worlds? Could these creatures be harmed by mere water?

The Darmarin, usually quick in its movements, had all but frozen because of her small spitting maneuver. Even though that hadn't been the most lady-like thing she'd ever done, Ayla found herself grateful for getting irritated enough to do such a thing. It might have saved her life.

Ayla pushed herself to her feet, standing ready to dodge any attack from the Darmarin. At least she wasn't in a helpless position now. Moreover, she had a secret weapon.

The Darmarin strafed nervously, keeping a small distance from Ayla. "What did you do? Human bodies produce such venom?"

"You wouldn't talk earlier, and now you expect me to reveal our secrets?" Ayla taunted. She had an ace up her sleeve now, something far more than just her mere ability to spit at the Darmarin, but if that kept the creature away from her while she figured out how to implement her plan, she was glad to have the threat.

Ayla reached inside her suit, grabbing for the small tube which connected and went along the neckline. There, she had a pouch full of drinking water meant as a backup in case she was stuck out somewhere for a long period of time. These environmental suits came in handy for staying alive, in more ways than the designers had intended.

She retrieved the tube and pointed it forward just out her neckline. It wasn't a pretty maneuver by any means, but all she had to do was get things right to defeat this creature.

"What are you doing?" the Darmarin asked, and as it did, it lunged for an attack, sensing that it had to move and act before matters got out of hand. It swiped its dangerous fingertips toward her again, and Ayla leaned backward, keeping her balance and making sure the tube pointed directly at the Darmarin's face.

She jammed her fist into her side where the pouch would have been, creating the pressure that would force the water up the tube without her having to suck on it. Water sprayed out of the tube and splashed at the Darmarin, hitting the creature directly in the face.

The alien recoiled, its entire facial structure seeming to melt off right in front of her. Ayla pressed forward as she had the advantage, jabbing her fist into the pouch area once again for another spray of water. This one hit the creature's head in the back of it. Its ridges melted away, as did skull structure, exposing brain tissue. The brain area throbbed, and Ayla backed off, hoping she did enough damage to finish the creature.

The Darmarin convulsed several times, gasping, reeling, and making strange sounds Ayla had never heard before. Then, after its melodramatic performance, the Darmarin collapsed to the floor.

Ayla waited several long moments while it didn't move. Finally, she stuck her toe out and lightly kicked at the alien. It remained slumped over, and her toe stung a little from hitting such a hard shell. The good news, however, was it was clearly dead. She'd thwarted the Darmarin, and now she could extract all of the data here and summon the pirates to pick her up.

She moved over to the console, tapping the controls to open up a comm line. "Ayla to *Peregrine*, come in."

"You're alive down there?" Mihael answered, sounding surprised.

"You don't give me enough credit," Ayla said. "I've dispatched our opposition. I can't say it was easy, but I'll survive, though I could use a good painkiller for my shoulder."

"I'm sure we've got something we can help you with," Mihael said.

"Anyway, it's clear here. You can send down a team. Definitely need Rams. We're going to want to carry this body back."

"Do I want to ask?"

Ayla couldn't help but look over at the dead alien on the floor. Her heart still raced seeing the thing, frightened from this new experience, something no one in humanity had ever seen before. There was other intelligent life out in the galaxy, something that would change the way the Imperium looked at the universe forever. But she would have to think of the repercussions of her discovery later. For now, she wanted to get back on the ship and collapse. "You'll definitely want to see this for yourself."

32

Ayla finished transporting the Darmarin's body into a small stasis container in the *Peregrine's* meager medical bay. She pretty much had to bend the thing in half in order to get it situated, the pirate vessel not equipped for hosting anything on this size of that lanky creature.

Mihael and Rams looked on as she finished her work. The pirate captain had brought along his security, perhaps not believing the Darmarin would be inanimate when they arrived. He had barked orders for the others to stay at their posts, though. With the ship still out in an asteroid field in this strange system, they needed to remain ready.

"That's it, huh?" Mihael asked.

"It is. And lasers do nothing against it," Ayla said, stepping toward the two pirates.

"Nothing?" Rams raised a brow. "Frightening."

"It's okay," Ayla said. "I found another weakness."

"Which is?"

"Classified for the time being. If we need it, I'll let you know." Ayla smiled. Even though a situation like this probably couldn't hurt to tell the pirates what she'd found, Terra Prime liked to keep their military information secret. Even though she liked these people, she wanted to observe some protocol.

"I don't feel right having one of those aboard the ship, all the same. Gives me the creeps," Mihael said.

"Me, too," Ayla admitted. They'd found aliens, hostile ones. Something that had never been discovered before. The prospect gave her the chills, and it was something she wouldn't get over any time soon.

"What now?" Mihael asked.

Ayla let out a small sigh. "Well, I wanted to hang around and help the resistance until the space Marines could get here. But I suppose now that we've discovered our friend here..." She motioned to the alien, "we should probably get the carcass back to Terra Prime for our analysts to get to work."

"I don't much want to go to the heart of the Imperium," Rams said, frowning.

"Don't worry," Ayla said. "You'll have immunity."

"So you say," Rams said.

"You know we can trust her." Mihael patted Rams on the shoulder. "Suits me fine enough. I want to get this creature off my ship as soon as I can anyway. Let's head to the bridge and get going."

As he finished his words, the ship rocked, lights flickering in the medical bay.

Ayla braced herself against the wall. "Asteroids?"

"I don't think so. Our deflector shielding should handle strays without that kind of reaction," Rams said.

"Let's hurry back." Mihael spun and picked up his pace for a swift walk through the ship to the bridge.

Ayla and Rams entered the bridge shortly behind the captain. Zahn scrambled at the piloting controls, and when they arrived, he merely pointed up to the viewer, which showed a giant, saucer-shaped object that radiated a column of light from beneath it, shining directly toward their ship.

Mihael turned pale white. This was no human ship, at least, no design Ayla had ever seen, and she was familiar with most of what the Imperium produced.

Given their captive, it could only mean one thing—Darmarin. And they probably weren't too happy with the events that had transpired in this asteroid field.

"The beam is draining our energy reserves," Zahn said. "I'm trying to get out of its way, but the beam seems to be slowing the ship somehow. I can't shake them." He kept scrambling at the controls, banking the ship, trying to move it away.

The lights dimmed again.

Darmarin sure enjoy absorbing energy, Ayla thought wryly. But what could she do about it?

"Don't hit them with lasers," Ayla said as Rams took his weapons controls. "They'll probably have ways to absorb those much like the creature did. Does the ship have projectiles?"

"We have two banks of hull-busters," Rams said.

Ships sometimes used those in combat to cut through the outer armor of a vessel so the lasers could penetrate more deeply. Two banks weren't much, but they would have to do if that was all they had.

"Better than nothing," Ayla said.

"Target?" Rams asked.

Ayla stared at the saucer on the screen. There wasn't much to look at other than a smooth surface. No real protrusions offering a clue as to where the ship's vital systems might be. The only differentiation was the light column targeting them. Ayla pointed to it. "Go right to the middle there. Let's see if we can break its hold."

Mihael nodded his agreement, quiet from his position, clearly unnerved by the existence of these aliens and their prowess.

Rams opened fire. The hull-busters darted from the ship, appearing on the screen along with smoke trails behind them. They headed straight for the alien vessel, which made no move to evade. They disappeared into the light column, and it was impossible to see if they connected or not.

Ayla held her breath. If those projectiles did nothing, they would surely be destroyed here. After all they'd fought and found, it could be meaningless if they couldn't get out of this system and back to Terra

Prime. The small pirate vessel just didn't have enough capabilities to take on such a threat.

Then, the light column flickered, much like the lights had inside the ship prior. Zahn turned the ship to the side, darting through the asteroid field and putting a good distance between them and the alien ship.

"Worked well enough," Zahn said.

"Get us out of here. As quickly as possible," Mihael said.

"I'm trying to. We need to shake them if we are going to get to a point where we can make a hyperspace jump out of here. I'm going to try to put a few asteroids in between us and the ship."

The *Peregrine* zigged and zagged through the asteroids, with a few larger rocks getting between them and the alien ship.

"I think we're in the clear. They haven't locked onto us," Zahn said.

As he spoke, the alien ship fired a thick beam, blasting a large asteroid into bits, removing any kind of barrier between the saucer and their meager vessel.

"Spoke too soon," Zahn said, scrambling and pushing the *Peregrine* to faster speeds.

"Hurry," Mihael said, clutching the arm rests of his captain's chair.

"I'm trying, but it'll do no good if we smash into one of the asteroids. We're almost clear of the field." Sweat dripped down the pilot's cheek and jawline, his facial expression tight with nerves.

Ayla braced herself along one of the rails at one of the back stations of the bridge. She had nothing she could do but hope the pirates could make it out of there. She hated being unable to act, helpless. Her job usually allowed her quite a bit of control of situations but, with this one, she had been at her colleagues' mercy on too many occasions. She couldn't wait for this assignment to end, but she hoped it wouldn't be at the end of an alien laser cannon.

The Darmarin saucer kept pace, busting through the asteroids with relentless persistence. It moved to destroy the rocks almost as quickly as the *Peregrine* could maneuver around them.

"How much farther until we can make the jump?" Mihael asked.

"We can do it now if you don't mind ending up smashed into an asteroid and ground into dust," Zahn said.

"Now's not the time for humor," Mihael said.

"Two, three minutes," Zahn said.

The *Peregrine* rocked as the alien saucer pelted it with a laser blast. It had caught up with them, passing the asteroids that Zahn had maneuvered between the two ships. His tactics were bound to work for only so long, especially as they came to the edge of the field where the space debris was sparser.

"Damage?" Mihael asked.

Rams looked down at his control console. "Grazed our outer hull. No breach that I can tell, but we can't take a lot of those hits."

Zahn zipped the ship around another sizable asteroid, and the Darmarin blasted it to bits as well, pushing right through. They looked like they were in the clear, but the alien ship was too close behind.

The column of light extended once again from the Darmarin vessel to the *Peregrine*, bringing the pirate vessel to a halt in space, and dimming the lights inside once again. They were trapped.

"Why aren't they just firing on us and ending us?" Ayla asked.

"Maybe they use this to charge their weapons and power the ship for the fight," Rams said.

It made sense. The Darmarin seemed to thrive off draining energy, almost like vampires. There would be no rush in killing them as they could drain all of the *Peregrine's* reserves first, which is what they seemed intent on doing.

"Power's down to forty percent," Rams said.

"Anything we can do?" Mihael asked. He looked back at Ayla, a desperate expression in his eyes.

Ayla wasn't sure how she could help. She didn't know the ins and outs of this ship. Rams would have known more, but they had already used their projectile weapons. Lasers would only feed the beast, so what else could they do?

"Do you have escape pods?" Ayla asked. Perhaps there was some potential way they could survive, if the aliens missed picking off the pods when they jettisoned from the *Peregrine*. It was better than sitting here and coming to a bitter end when power gave out.

"No, we don't," Mihael said. "This isn't a luxury barge, it's a pirate ship."

Pirates didn't tend to be the most safety conscious of people, though Ayla wanted to smack Mihael upside the head for not having standard escape pods aboard. Space could be a dangerous place, and there was no reason to completely risk everyone's lives aboard like this. What on Terra Prime had he been thinking when he set sail with this ship?

All Ayla could do was shake her head.

Mihael pressed his lips together, forehead wrinkling in consternation. "It was nice knowing all of you. I appreciate having flown with you."

Rams pounded his fist on his console, which chirped in protest as he had hit some control or another. "No. Not like this."

The lights dimmed again, the viewer winking out and giving them no more vision of what lay beyond in space. They were sitting ducks now.

Power came back on briefly, though the lights were dimmer than before. Nothing was on the screen still.

Several moments passed, ones in which they should have lost power again and life support systems along with it. Ayla glanced between the others.

"Any idea what's happening?" Zahn asked.

Rams cleared his control panel, which winked on and off several times. They only had so much in their power reserves. "I'm trying to get a clear picture. It looks like there's other vessels out there. Our flying saucer has peeled off us."

If the saucer no longer targeted them, it could only mean one thing —the Imperial Space Fleet was there with the Marines. Ayla perked, finally with some good news.

"Get a message out, quickly!" Ayla said. "Let them know to use projectiles only."

Zahn tapped at the comm. "Trying. It's hard to get a signal."

"Shut down non-essential systems," Mihael said.

"Working on it," Rams said.

Zahn kept working the comm. "I got it. Message is out." He leaned back in his chair.

They waited again as the bridge fell into silence. They were blind, unable to see out into space. How many fleet ships were out there? They had no way of knowing. It had to be enough to deal with one of these alien ships.

"The saucer is no longer showing any energy readings," Rams said. He looked up toward Mihael, relief on his face. "I think they've destroyed it."

"God bless the emperor," Ayla said, happy her faith in her Imperium had paid off for them.

"Send them out another distress signal," Mihael said, "and let them know we'll need a tow." He leaned back into his seat and let out a giant sigh of relief.

33

THE I.S.S. *EXCALIBUR* BROUGHT IN THE *PEREGRINE* TO CONNECT WITH its docking port, extending an arm that covered the back of the pirate ship's cargo exit to allow their bay doors to open into an area with full atmosphere.

The pirates gathered down in the bay, Jannik opening the doors and allowing the imperials to gain access to the ship. The ramp descended just like when they were landed, but opening into a small corridor, all white with bright lights inside.

A dozen space Marines stood in formation with laser rifles pointed into the pirate ship.

Ayla's heart pounded, seeing the immediate danger of the situation. To the space Marines, the crew of the *Peregrine* were still pirates to be dealt with. There hadn't been time nor communication to explain the situation. Their coming in guns blazing could end in a tragic loss of life if matters weren't deescalated quickly.

She held her arms up. "Hold your fire!" Ayla said.

The Marines were in complete combat armor, faces covered by helmets that sealed them into their environmental suits. The gray armor added an additional layer of protection which would keep them safer from laser blasts than if they wore standard space gear.

"Hands where we can see them," one of the Marines shouted, ignoring that Ayla already had her hands up.

"Do as they say," Mihael said, raising his own hands. "We don't need to get killed by some trigger-happy soldiers."

The pirates grudgingly complied with their captain.

The space Marines, meanwhile, moved forward and disarmed the pirates, taking weapons from holsters at their belts, as well as patting them down to remove other weaponry. They did the same with Ayla, clearly not recognizing who she was.

"I need to speak with your commander," Ayla said. "I'm special agent Ayla Rin of Terra Prime. I have an ident code and clearance to confirm my identity."

The soldier who patted her down stopped and looked at her through his helmet. "Lieutenant," he called.

The original Marine who spoke stepped toward Ayla. "You claim to be an imperial agent?" he asked. "What are you doing all the way out here, and why are you on a pirate ship?"

They were valid questions and matters Ayla wouldn't discuss with ordinary soldiers. "I'm afraid those matters are classified. I'm happy to present you with my credentials, as I said. This crew with me has immunity granted by the agency, so tell your men to be careful with how they treat them."

"We'll see if your story pans out," the lieutenant said.

Ayla was taken away from the rest of the group, down the corridor and into the *Excalibur*. There, she was grilled by officers who took her ident information and clearance codes, confirmed with retinal scans and thumbprints while leaving her in a room by herself. The confirmation process took several minutes, but Ayla remained calm, sitting with her hands folded over a table while the military men came back. When they did, they opened the door.

"Your story checks out," the lieutenant said.

"Of course. Now, as far as the pirates, I'm hoping you can give their ship a little recharge and send them about their merry way," Ayla said.

"These people are wanted on seven counts of—"

Ayla held her hand up. "Immunity, remember? It's emperor-level override. All of their crimes will be commuted."

The lieutenant tightened his face and grumbled. "I lost several good men to pirates in the Battle of Okenfold."

Ayla met his eyes trying to look reassuring. "I sympathize for your loss. These aren't the same people responsible, though. You'll have to trust me that they've done service to the Imperium warranting their release."

The lieutenant glanced to the side, becoming distant for a moment before he nodded. "Very well. If they have immunity, we'll do as you say. Anything else you'd like us to know before we settle matters planetside?"

"I'll leave all that to you," Ayla said, giving the lieutenant a warm smile. "I'm going to requisition a hyperspace-capable shuttle from you and be on the first flight back home to Terra Prime, if it's all the same."

"You've got quite the clearance level, missy," the lieutenant said. "It says here we're supposed to follow your every command. I've never seen anything like it before."

"And if all goes well enough, you never will again. Thank you for your service, lieutenant."

The officer led Ayla out of the interrogation room.

EPILOGUE

Ayla watched a feed of a science lab, men in white coats and goggles dissecting the lanky alien she had encountered on the asteroid. It was a gruesome sight, watching a creature get pulled apart and prodded by different scientific instruments, but it was also one of the biggest discoveries mankind had ever made.

The public didn't know about it yet. Emperor Grigor had called in his advisory committee and determined they shouldn't leak information about the existence of extraterrestrials until they had a solid plan on how to handle them.

One thing was clear, the Darmarin were enemies of the Imperium. They had hatched a plan to try to strip mankind of its humanity, of its memories, the very thing that separated man from animal. If Ayla and her pirate friends hadn't helped put a stop to it, it could have exported to trillions of souls across the galaxy.

All in a day's work for her.

She crossed her arms, continuing to watch the feed as Jorus grabbed a bottle of some amber liquid and poured a drink for himself.

"Want a glass?" he asked. "This is a pretty rare bottle from a distillery on Beta Proxima. I've heard it fetches quite a few Grigorums in back markets."

Ayla gave him a small smile. "You know I don't like to drink much, but I'll have a sip and try it." She held up her thumb and index finger nearly pinched together to show him she only wanted a small amount.

Jorus poured the drink and set it on the desk in front of her. "The agency is about turned upside down with the news you found. I still don't know what to make of these Darmarin. We have too many worlds on the fringes where we don't have a strong Imperial presence to be able to catch these kinds of machinations."

"That's what you have me for." Ayla took the drink into her hand, bringing her nose to the rim of the glass and inhaling to get a scent. It smelled of nuts and strong alcohol, nothing surprising to her, but she held off on taking a sip.

On the viewer, men dug into the alien's body with scalpels and other instruments. With the hard exoskeleton, it took some doing to get past the surface, but they continued to work.

"I doubt we're going to see much going on here. Would you mind?" Jorus asked, motioning to the off button of the viewer.

"Doesn't matter to me." Ayla took a sip of the liquid, which tasted as strong as it smelled.

"Thank you. I've never been a fan of medical procedures. Makes me squeamish. You think I'd be a little more desensitized given our line of work." Jorus shrugged.

"We all have our quirks," Ayla said. She could tell Jorus felt uncomfortable, and so she deftly changed the subject. "How is the reconstruction going on Zenda?"

"The space Marines secured the major cities within several hours of their arrival," Jorus said. "Colonel Okamoto reports that the populace really didn't offer much resistance to their control. The members of the council who were working with the alien influence have been detained and are awaiting trial for treason to the Imperium." Jorus sipped his drink casually as if such matters were all in a small day's work. In some ways, they were, though with the extraterrestrial involvement, this was no routine mission.

"What about Hervey?"

"Your contact from the groundside resistance?" Jorus asked.

Ayla nodded. There were so many people who helped her on this last mission, but she felt a lot of compassion for Hervey and the situation he had with his wife. She still shivered every time she thought about the prospect of losing a loved one in such a gruesome manner, all memory stripped. It was like their lives together never occurred.

"From the reports I read, our military peacekeepers and agents contacted him once on the ground. He's not the friendliest of allies, preferring to not have our teams involved in the governance of this world. Were you aware of that?"

Ayla gave Jorus a soft smile. "Not everyone's perfect. Without having much contact from the Imperium for hundreds of years, you can see why someone would want to be more independently driven from a perspective. He's reasonable, though. He'll come around in time."

"I hope so, or we might get some flak from the higher ups," Jorus said. "We're trusting you on this because of the word you put in."

"Have I ever steered you wrong before?" Ayla asked.

"No, but it doesn't mean you get carte blanche to install whatever leadership you want on any planet. There's still limits, and we're beholden to the emperor."

Ayla held her hands up innocently. "I wouldn't have it any other way."

She could joke around with Jorus to some degree because he knew she was loyal to both Emperor Grigor and the Imperium as a whole. So was he. Their mutual values made it easy to work with one another for the most part, though Ayla really needed a break after these last two missions.

Going from backwater planet to backwater planet on difficult assignments took a toll on her. Both planets had a mad leadership trying to brainwash their populations, albeit by different means and to different ends. The sights she'd seen over the last couple of months were so bizarre, she wouldn't be able to tell stories about it even if she was allowed to talk about the classified matters.

She looked forward to getting back to her garden on Terra Prime.

She didn't have a large plot of land to grow her plants and flowers, but it was enough to give her a little peace when she had time to be home. With her being away for so long, she had to pay one of the neighbor kids to tend to her plants, hoping they would take decent enough care of them that her garden wouldn't be withered and dead upon her return. Kids could only be trusted so far, and she hadn't been able to check back in on them, though she'd asked Jorus to do so on her behalf.

He also could only be trusted to do so much, since the man was preoccupied with his work more often than not, just as she could be.

Right now, he had a preoccupation with his drink as he kept placing his nose close to the top of the glass and inhaling, closing his eyes. He muttered something about complex flavors but seemed to be more into his own experience in fine spirits than their conversation debriefing the mission.

"Well, it sounds like everything's in order," Ayla said, taking a small sip from her glass. "I'm glad we were able to stop the production of this immortality spore. Did our teams find any way to reverse the effects?"

Jorus shook his head. "Nothing yet. We have a full medical unit detached to Zenda, but it's going to take some time for them to analyze all of the spore's properties and see if they can undo the damage. Hundreds of thousands of people now have memory loss conditions because of what was done there. Absolutely atrocious. But we'll do what we can. The Imperium always does."

Even though no system of government was perfect, the Imperium always moved toward what it believed to be right, which is what comforted Ayla about all of the hard jobs and dirty work she had to do much of the time. Sometimes, people got hurt, or killed. She'd lost enough colleagues and informants over her modest couple of years of service thus far, and she imagined those numbers would continue to compound over the next several years. But their deaths wouldn't be in vain, and she would remember the sacrifices made, even if no one else did. Speaking of sacrifices…

"Oh, and the pirates who assisted me? They were left alone, and their crimes were commuted formally, yes?"

"The agency really doesn't appreciate you making those kind of promises," Jorus said in a warning tone.

"Jorus, you promised—"

He waved off her concern. "I did, and the Imperium always delivers on promises. Sometimes, they take more time than not but, in this instance, your friends were sent about on their merry way."

Ayla let out a sigh of relief, letting her shoulders relax into her chair. She'd been concerned about Mihael and the others. For all they were pirates, they were good people, and they helped her without questioning too many of her orders and suggestions. Such loyal people were hard to find in the universe, and probably even harder to find among their cohorts. She wanted the best for them, and though she recognized once she had gotten aboard the Imperial cruiser that she wouldn't be able to return to their ranks even to say goodbye, she was glad to know that her people took care of the promises to keep them from prison or worse.

"I still think we should have given them a reward for their service," Ayla said.

"Don't push it."

"Fair enough." Ayla set down her glass on Jorus's desk and stood. "Well, that should be everything. Thank you for the delightful sampling. I should be heading back to my place to check on my plants."

Jorus looked up with her with a twinkle in his eye. "You mean, you're not ready to depart on your next mission?"

"You can't do that to me. I'm due some leave!" Ayla protested.

Her handler laughed at the reaction, downing the rest of the liquid in his glass. "You're too easy to rattle. I thought we trained you better than that. No, you'll have a bit of leave, but the emperor is having a round table banquet in two days' time, and you've been requested to join."

The emperor wanted her to join one of his meetings with his advisors? They were framed as banquets, but from what Ayla understood, a lot of Imperial policy was made and decided at these round tables. She perked up, surprised that she was getting a personal invitation to the most important table in the galaxy. Her heart fluttered with the idea of being able to speak with Emperor Grigor at length about ideas for a more perfect Imperium.

"You can count on me to be there."

APPENDIX A

Ayla Rin: Origin

Bright lights blinked in Ayla's face at such incredible speeds her mind whirled. Patterns, shapes, they all came into her view.

Rapid learning machines weren't legal in the Imperium, except under strict government control. It gave lords and bureaucrats an advantage over the average populace, suppressing their ability to learn —or at least the ones who didn't get chosen for special programs.

There were risks to such machines, of course. One in three hundred minds burned out when subjected to such rigorous data entry directly into the brain.

But she had the aptitude, and the doctors in charge of the project told her she didn't exhibit any of the signs of problems from learning.

It was too late to change her mind now. Each repetition of the lights blinked faster and brighter. Soon, her mind succumbed to their power. Everything dissipated into a wash of brightness beyond anything she'd ever seen before.

"Are you okay?" a voice summoned her back to reality.

Ayla blinked several times, the world becoming less fuzzy around her and giving her a view of her surroundings.

She lay in a lab on a biobed cocked forty-five-degrees, with a doctor staring at her, along with Jorus, the man from the Terra Prime Intelligence Agency.

He'd been the one to recruit her, to bring her here. She trusted him a lot. For all she knew, all of this could be fake, some kind of test.

"Ayla?" Jorus asked.

"I'm fine. My eyes are adjusting to the light."

The lab came into full view, all of the instruments, lights, panels, she could see everything. The procedure must have been a success. Her brain couldn't have burned out and returned like this.

"Are you in possession of all of your faculties, Ms. Rin?" the doctor asked.

Ayla wiggled her fingertips and dropped her chin. She could move her legs as well. Everything seemed in order. "I think I'm okay."

"And what of your new learning?" Jorus asked.

"Give it time," the doctor said. "She has to process all—"

Before he could finish his words, the doors to the lab whooshed open.

Three men dressed in all black, wearing masks and black caps entered. They held ray guns in their hands. The one distinguishing mark they held was a red scorpion embroidered across their chests.

Ayla recognized them, though she didn't know where she'd come across the information. It must have been part of the learning.

The Scorpions came from the Scorpio constellation, colonies along each of the planetoids and asteroids in the sector. Their primary aim was to incite rebellion and achieve independence for the Scorpio Constellation from the Imperium.

They had to be stopped.

Easier said than done when laser blasts came firing out of their ray guns.

The doctor became the first casualty, getting scorched by their ray guns before he could move.

Jorus was faster. He ducked behind a piece of lab equipment on wheels, and then pushed it toward one of the attackers. Caught off guard, the attacker got hit by the equipment, and then stumbled backward until his head slammed against the wall of instruments behind him. He crumpled to the floor.

It left two of them.

One trained his ray gun on Ayla. He fired.

A laser struck, but Ayla rolled out of the way. The blast tore apart the biobed. Foam flew everywhere, and a large scorch mark lay where Ayla's head had been a moment prior. She'd barely survived.

Ayla's heart raced. She had to move quickly.

The Scorpio terrorist kept firing his gun, edging closer to her. Ayla managed to dodge each shot. She had a sense of where he would fire before he pulled the trigger.

It gave her an advantage.

Her learning kicked in. Ayla's eyes went wide as a whole array of martial arts and tactics opened to her mind.

These men no longer seemed a threat.

Ayla cartwheeled toward her attacker, her feet connecting with the ray gun when she came close enough to strike him. It flew from the man's hand.

When she landed on her feet, he delivered a right hook toward her.

Ayla managed to duck the blow, bringing her own uppercut to the attacker's chin.

He stumbled backward, but her lithe frame couldn't deliver a knockout blow in one hit.

Before he could recover, Ayla delivered a flurry of punches to him, driving him backward and into the other Scorpio terrorist who was now engaged with Jorus.

The two collided, crumpling to the floor atop the third of their Scorpio attackers.

Jorus had his fists up, breathing hard. He looked at her and nodded approvingly. "I see your learning went well."

Ayla laughed. "I know Kung Fu!" she exclaimed. She could hardly believe it.

Jorus laughed along with her.

Later, Ayla sat in Jorus's office, a quaint space in a non-descript building. Somewhere perfect to conduct operations for Terran Intelligence without anyone bothering them.

She had her arms crossed as Jorus logged the report of the day's events.

"Now you understand what we're up against," Jorus said. "When I came across your aptitude testing numbers, I didn't come to you because I thought it would be a great job for a decent payroll, nor that it would give you any societal advancement." He turned toward her. "Don't get me wrong, being an Agent of Terra Prime has its perks. You'll find the credit account while on assignment to be tempting to say the least. But we also deal with threats every day."

"I thought it was some simulated test," Ayla said. She still didn't believe random agents from the Scorpio Constellation could have broken into the government medical facility. Was security truly so lax? What better way did they have to test a potential new agent? And also to get rid of the one witness who knew anything about her.

Jorus raised a brow but ignored her comment. "Regardless, there is danger. You've got all the best training we can offer. Do you think you're ready?"

"As I'll ever be," Ayla said. "What's next?"

Jorus: Origin
  Co-Written with Queenie

I.

A multitude of dots lit on a map, one blinking faster than another, with little beeps sounding to alert anyone nearby. The room was empty besides the one person sitting slouched into a chair, Emperor Grigor VI of the Terran Imperium. He raised a hand to the bridge of his nose as his other hand gave a small wave, barely moving it as if the mere motion proved too much work.

The beeping stopped, silence blanketing over the room. Grigor stood, pacing around the map with the lit dots. A collective of seven or eight dots flickered in red light across the holographic map. Though sporadically spread out before him, it was a headache to witness. The silence was finally broken with a patterned bell chiming, an announcement of an arrival.

"Enter," Grigor said. The doors swept open as if by some sort of invisible hand. The emperor could not help but feel a ripple of relaxation flow over his body as he opened his arms in a welcoming fashion, beckoning for the man standing there. One of his most trusted advisors strode into the room, with a blank expression on his face. His right arm raised up to his left shoulder as he dipped his head in greeting. The lanky man liked to be called Drake, eschewing formalities of last names or positions.

"Emperor, you called?" His voice was slow, controlled, and monotone, almost like a robot. His response took the same time as required to lift himself back up as Grigor took the few steps required to approach the table, motioning for his Advisor to join him. The man took his slow steps over, following as the emperor obeyed.

"Yes, you know of all the issues the Imperium is currently presented with, of course. Who among us is not? However, it is beyond the scope of a simple mission to fix it, when one goes down another four more pop up. It's time for this to come to an end."

"And what do you have in mind, Emperor, to fix such issues?" Drake's monotone voice was quick to chime in as he wandered around the table. Almost as if on cue, another light blinked. The emperor gave the signal for the obnoxious alert to silence before he responded.

"That's where you come in. You must be able to create a solution for such an issue." Grigor raised an eyebrow with a small smile rising on his lips.

Drake gave a sharp nod of his head.

"Out of, how you so kindly put it, my experience, my best advice for such a large task at hand would include creating a collective, an agency if you will, specifically entrusted in being able to handle such. It would definitely take someone at the top of their field, with skill and talent that is not easily found in others."

"I take it you already have someone in mind?"

"I do, but this is a task that requires perfection. I have the perfect candidate, but one can never be too cautious. With your permission, Emperor, I would like to run, shall we say a test. This agency requires secrecy and requires a certain level of abilities. I would relish in a world where such loyalty to the Imperium is natural, yet one can never take too many precautions."

"Do what you must with whatever resources you require. Whatever it takes, as long as it gets rid of the problems. You are dismissed, take care of the issue." With the dismissal, Drake did not give a verbal response. He raised his arm across his heart once more as his head dipped while backing out of the room, his head returning to be held high as he headed away for his mission.

II.

Drake wasted no time as he made his way toward where his prime pick of a leader would be. He made a single stop to venture for a certain object which found a home in his sleeve. A few short minutes later, he had arrived at his destination. As expected, Jorus was within his office, working on some new paperwork. Drake had little care in what the paperwork was actually for as he strode into the room. Jorus glanced at Drake, raising an eyebrow in questioning.

"How may I be of service?" he asked as he put his attention back down toward his papers, expecting this to be a simple visit or a courtesy call. He had been quite busy but always ready to be of service to the Imperium.

"I have a job for you," Drake said. "I have a rather special delivery that requires an escort. I do not have faith in any normal being to take this to its destination."

"And you wish for me to escort this delivery for you?" Jorus asked. "And what is it that you wish for me to escort?"

"We have a chip," Drake said, holding up a small data crystal and setting it down on the table before Jorus. "The information within is not something a simple pilot or even respectable soldier would be trusted with. Should this information reach its destination, it would be a great help in dealing with the unrest that plagues the Imperium. It would be too obvious for someone like me to take it, that is too great of a risk and too much of a journey should the emperor require me. I trust that you, of all people, would be able to make such a mission with ease and discretion."

Jorus could not argue with that logic. In fact, he could not deny any of the praise that Drake had offered to him. However, he still had one more question. "And, Sir, where would this destination be?"

"Ymir." Not a far distance, but not exactly a walk down the block, either. The planet would be about a day and a half ride along a starcruiser. "We need this delivered as soon as possible."

"I shall see to it right away."

"Wonderful. Safe travels, my friend. Make the Imperium proud." Drake's final words were strong as he took the clue to leave the crystal on the table and wasted no time walking out of the room. Jorus was unable to give a response as Drake's departure was swift, but his eyes left the back of Drake's leaving form to glance toward the crystal that was left on his desk.

Jorus reached for the crystal, picking up the baseball-sized shining orb. With a simple twist, it opened to reveal a chip, which contained the unknown, yet apparently saving, information. He twisted it shut, the locks *clicking* into place as he slid the crystal into his pocket before leaving his office. A starcruiser was set to leave soon, and he would be aboard.

His trip to the docking station was a quick one with no detours. Not a single possible distraction could take Jorus from his mission. It should be, and in his mind would be, swiftly executed. Of course, just a quick word with the pilot ensured there would be a stop at Ymir so Jorus would be able complete his mission and hopefully return right home. All was perfect till someone crashed into him.

III.

Colliding with Jorus, the other person lost their footing. Jorus, however, with his bigger build, remained safely standing on both feet. Before the other could hit the ground, Jorus caught the figure before gravity could do its damage.

"Oh, my. I wasn't looking where I was going, I am so, so sorry. Please," a frantic female voice filled the awkward silence that had dominated the distance between the two people. Word after word streamed from her mouth as she patted down her hair.

"It is all right. No harm was done," Jorus cut off the woman before she could sink further into her panic and worry.

She smoothed her black skirt to adjust any wrinkles formed from the fumble. Then, she returned to a poised position.

"I do apologize. I was in a rush to make it aboard and was worried the starcruiser would have left without me." She held her shoulders back and lifted her chin so she could meet Jorus's eyes.

Jorus shifted his hands back to his side. "I appreciate the apology. You did no harm, so there's no foul."

She held up a hand to him. "Eveline. It's a pleasure to meet you though I wish this was under better circumstances. Please, allow me to make up for this. Won't you join me for a drink perhaps?"

A drink? The starcruiser did have a rather luxurious bar aboard, and it was a bit of a distance to Ymir. There was no harm in a little relaxation.

"The pleasure is all mine. Please, call me Jorus. I would be more than happy to join you. That sounds lovely." He lifted his hand to meet hers in the formal greeting. Her ivory skin was flawless and smooth while his hand was calloused. His scars each had a story while the only noticeable parts of her hands were the decorative rings she wore. Eveline smiled, her teeth showing as her lips parted as she nodded with her head for them to venture deeper into the starcruiser.

The starcruiser was equipped with a rather extensive number of luxuries, from a variety of shops and restaurants to even entertainment. The pair, however, headed for the central attraction of the cruiser—the full-service bar. Drinks, food, music, the starcruiser had it all. With the popularity of the place, it took the pair some time hovering around stools to find seats. Groups of beings gathered in different sections, often centralized around many of the serving bars. Once settled comfortably and orders placed, Jorus moved into conversation with the woman.

"What's led someone like you to be on a starcruiser headed out toward Ymir?"

Eveline's eyes cast down at her cup. She glanced up through her lashes to smile at Jorus. "My current employer has asked that I aid a few co-workers who are currently working on a project in Ymir. Why pass up a fully sponsored travel trip?" A little giggle slipped through her lips. "What about you? Why did I get the pleasure of meeting such a fine gentleman?"

"Business. Nothing too exciting," Jorus said.

"Are you alone, then? That's boring. I could never dream of working alone."

"My job often entails some alone time, though I have learned to enjoy it by now."

"No one should have to enjoy that much alone time. Your job must be very worth it for you to endure such suffering." Her soft tone sounded sincere. She was coming onto him, clearly, but why?

"There is no need, I am quite comfortable, besides, it is those I meet at times like these make it less lonely." A tint of red was visible on Eveline's cheeks as she chuckled, brushing some of her hair out of her face.

Words flowed as the drinks piled upon the table, and soon enough, the two shared more than cordial quips. Eveline's soft giggles turned into more genuine laughter as Jorus allowed himself to take a breath and enjoy the time with the woman. Words turned into soft touches on the arm, followed by Eveline's head leaning against his arm as they spoke. A small altercation with someone attempting to touch Eveline's back led to Jorus putting a strong arm around her as they continued to drink and converse. Before they knew it, time was gone.

"My goodness, I didn't even realize how late it became." Eveline's shock broke through their shared laughter. "I should get to bed."

"Come, I'll walk you back to your room. There's no need for you to go alone."

No objections followed as Jorus helped the girl down from her chair. They went on a casual stroll through the starcruiser toward her room, and she motioned toward the higher end quarters with a nod of her head. Soon, they made it inside her cabin. Jorus hovered by the door as Eveline sauntered.

She turned to him with a bright smile on her face. "There's no need for you to leave so soon."

IV.

Her words enticed him. Jorus took a deep breath, considering what would occur. His rational thinking didn't get far before a mix of the alcohol and Eveline taking his arm pulled him from his thoughts and deeper into the room, the door closing behind him. Her hand brought him back to the present of him, this woman, and the rest of the night. He pulled her close, his figure towering over hers as he took control of the situation.

The dim lighting made the mood crystal clear as his fingers made quick work of her blouse buttons. Undoing each one took all but a second, but he made it so painfully slow as to draw quiet whimpers from her lips. Finally, the white fabric was let open to reveal a dark brassiere beneath. Their smiles matched one another as lips met lips, her hands tugging at the end of his uniformed shirt.

"Come on, let's get comfy," she purred between kisses. Eveline led him to a back bedroom through another set of doors.

Before Jorus could thoroughly enjoy the situation, the world became hazy, and he lost consciousness. He sat up on the bed, alone in the dark, hearing rustling coming from the main room.

He heard footsteps, paired with a frustrated sigh, and his entire mood shifted to alertness. He scrambled to his feet and opened the door.

Eveline kneeled on the floor, her white shirt pulled over her upper body to cover her, sifting through Jorus's discarded clothing. Her eyes shot up to his, fear present in her expression as she realized she'd been caught. She rose to her feet, attempting to take a few steps back.

Jorus was too fast for her, grabbing her wrist, stopping her from getting farther. A yell escaped her lips as she attempted to pull away, however, Jorus was in no mood to deal with it.

"What were you doing?" he demanded, his eyes narrowing.

"Nothing. let me go!" Her attempts to fight back were useless. His stone-cold look bored deep into her eyes as he attempted to piece together what she had been attempting to extract from him. With his foot, he kicked up his clothing that she had been rummaging through. With one hand holding Eveline's wrists, he used the other to sift through till he found his prized possession. The crystal was still safe, still secure.

"I'll let you go when you tell me what you wanted." His voice was low, controlled, yet furious as the words hissed between his teeth. She shook her head as she refused to reply. "No answer, that's fine. You're under arrest in the name of the Imperium."

"No, please! I don't know much!" The simple threat of arrest was the cherry on top to send her over the edge as tears spilled from those once gorgeous eyes.

"What do you know?!"

"I was hired, but they didn't give me a name. It's what I do. They identify a person, what they want from him, and how to drop off the goods. I never see who hires me, and I never know what they do with what they want. Usually, it's just to distract someone, throw them off course."

"That doesn't answer the question! What did you want from me?" Jorus's patience ran thin as he knew full well what she aimed to extract, but he wanted confirmation.

"Some crystal! I don't know for whom or what it does. They gave me your name, picture, and told me you had some crystal they wanted!" the words spilled from her mouth as Jorus froze. He had no words, his mind empty. It was for all but a split second as he pushed Eveline back, her body falling onto one of the plush couches of the room. He wasted no time in putting his clothing back on.

"I should have you arrested, executed, or abandoned on some planet where you would never be found. But because I'm a nice person, consider this your warning. I have your picture, your fingerprints, anything needed to ID you. Take a job like this ever again, and it will be the last job you take."

Eveline shook, her entire body quivering so her nod was barely evident through the constant movement. Jorus didn't bother to look at her again as he strode out of the room, his hands balled in fists as if ready to swing at anyone who crossed in front of him. Of course, it had been a trap. He felt stupid for nearly falling for her.

V.

Jorus's face fell to a scowl as he realized it was the early morning. He had all but a handful of hours till his arrival at Ymir, and he had little interest in returning to his quarters. He found himself at one of the restaurants, enjoying a simple meal. The crystal never left his pocket, and he was now hyper-aware of its additional weight. Sure enough, the morning went by, and the cruiser made its arrival to Ymir. Jorus joined the queue of those disembarking and made note that Eveline was not among them. Smart girl.

Jorus strode off the cruiser and into the port, glancing around. He hadn't been given instructions on what to do upon arrival.

Nearby, he found a gathering of men in uniform standing guard outside a building. He entered, his credentials allowing him access and, within, was none other than Drake, the Imperial advisor, seated at a table with a plate of food before him.

Jorus raised an eyebrow as Drake raised his hands in greeting, a muffled hello being called out as his mouth was full. After a swig of water, Drake stood to greet Jorus.

"You made it! Fantastic!"

"Yes, I made it. Why are you here? Couldn't you have taken the crystal if you were headed this direction?"

"Oh, don't worry about that. Do you have it?"

"Of course, I do." Jorus was still a little bewildered why Drake had come to Ymir. He produced the crystal from his pocket, placing it on the table before Drake.

"No trouble I take it?" Drake asked as he picked up the crystal, inspecting it.

"Nothing I couldn't handle. Some agency sent a thief after me. I am curious as to how they knew what I was carrying," Jorus said.

Drake let out a low chuckle. Once content with his inspection, he placed the crystal in a case, and then handed it to a guard, who walked off with it. Jorus, confused, opened his mouth to question, but Drake spoke first.

"Jorus, the Imperium has a question for you."

"Imperium or Emperor?"

"Emperor Grigor asking for the Imperium as a whole."

"What is the question?"

"How much are you willing to do for this Imperium?"

Jorus had never been more confused by a sequence of events. He had dedicated his entire life of service to the Imperium, what would he not do?

"Why, what kind of question is that? You have access to my records."

"Then you know of the wave of insurgences occurring across the whole of the Imperium."

"Of course, I do. Who doesn't?" It was simple knowledge for someone like him. He attempted to keep a close eye on the traitors, where they were, who financed them. It was important information to know for a position like his.

"Emperor Grigor has asked me to aid in forming a group—an agency if you will—tasked with dealing with these issues."

"And what's that do with me? I can offer recommendations of those I have worked with who would be good," Jorus offered as he racked his brain for those he thought would do well in this type of work.

"Jorus, we're asking that you head the group. You obviously have the skill. You made it here despite the difficulties, even the most complicated one I could find."

"What do you mean *you* could find?"

"Don't you see? This was all a test. We were the ones who sent Trella, or you know her as Eveline. Her charms didn't work on you. We know you have utmost loyalty." A test? Eveline, or whatever Drake had said her name was?

"You needed to test me?" the words came out indignant as he was justifiably upset at this news. He hadn't dedicated his life to servicing the Imperium to have his abilities and loyalties tested.

"It was a precaution, Jorus, but it does not matter. You passed. And now you are ready to take on your next stage of service, heading this agency to deal with our galactic problems."

He regained his composure. This was an honor despite the indignancy of the last several hours. "I shall gladly do so; it would be an honor to serve the Imperium in such a way." With a dip of his head in respect, he accepted his new position. It was a privilege to be chosen for such a job, and Jorus was sure to do everything within his power to do it well.

"Wonderful. Join me, and we shall return to the Emperor to get started."

ALSO BY JON DEL ARROZ

THE ADVENTURES OF BARON VON MONOCLE:
For Steam And Country
The Blood Of Giants
The Fight For Rislandia
The Iron Wedding
The Steam Knight

THE NANO TEMPLAR Series
Justified
Sanctified
Glorified

THE ARYSHAN WAR
The Stars Entwined
The Stars Asunder
The Stars Rejoined
Colony Launch

www.ingramcontent.com/pod-product-compliance
Lightning Source LLC
Chambersburg PA
CBHW031237210726

48287CB00003B/801